MW01076961

For everyone who never gives up.
For the love of Odin, you've got this.

RAIDHO
JOURNEY
PROGRESS · GROWTH · THE PATH

I

REYNA

My head was spinning as I whirled around the empty room.

How had this happened?

Kara's book lay open on the floor, Lhoris' pipe on the arm of the chair he had been sitting in when I last saw them.

Tears swam across my vision, born more of rage than of sorrow.

Who had taken my friends?

They were supposed to be safe here. Ellisar had been guarding them.

Ellisar.

The fleeting memory of the big man on the floor of the sitting room forced its way through the clanging panic in my head.

I ran back to the main room and saw Frima heaving his large body over.

"Come on, talk to me, you big lummox," she muttered.

He was bleeding from a cut on his forehead, but his chest was moving.

"Guards," he mumbled, and Frima cast her eyes upward, murmuring thanks to the gods.

I moved to them, dropping to a crouch.

"Which guards?"

"Queen's," he sighed, his eyes opening a crack. "My head..." They rolled back, showing his irises, and Frima tapped her hands on his cheeks firmly.

"Reyna, get brandy, now."

I did as she asked, moving to the drinks cabinet on the far wall. My hands trembled as I clumsily poured the drink.

If he was right and the Queen's guards had taken my friends... They were *gold-givers*. The most valuable tools of her sworn enemy.

Swallowing down my fear, I returned with the drink. Frima had pulled Ellisar up to lean against her side, and she took the glass from me.

"His wound is not serious, he has little blood loss. Just a severe blow to the head," she said quietly to me.

Ellisar lifted one hand, then blinked down at it. "Why is it blue?"

Frima snarled and swore. "A *very* severe blow to the head."

"Ellisar, why did the Queen's guards take my friends?" I tried to keep the urgency out of my voice and speak to the injured man calmly. I failed.

He looked dazedly up at me. "The woman wrote something down," he slurred.

I dropped to my knees. "Where? Where did she write it?"

His gaze dropped to his chest, and Frima and I both followed it. A piece of paper was pinned to the inside of his furs, the edge poking out.

I snatched it up.

"As a celebration of the end of the Shadow Court's hosting of the *Leikmot*, you are cordially invited to a masked ball at midnight tonight," I read. "In order to provide entertainment fitting for such an event, each of our champions has had something precious taken from them. The opportunity to win them back will take place at the ball. Regards, the Shadow Court Crown."

Frima took the paper from me before I could screw it up. Rage was causing black dots to float at the edges of my vision, and my mouth was as dry as a sand.

"Hasn't she fucking done enough?"

"Calm down. This means they're still alive," Frima answered, scanning the note.

I clung to her words.

They were still alive.

But the Queen was crazy. Completely unhinged. Could she be trusted to keep them alive until midnight?

And besides, alive did not mean unharmed.

I spun on my heel, heading for the open door. "Reyna, where are you going? Without Maz here you can't—"

"I can, and I fucking will."

I didn't stay to listen to her protest.

An unexpected burst of anger with Mazrith was coursing through me.

This wouldn't have happened if he hadn't left. The Queen would never have been so bold as to break into his rooms.

Well, I may not have his power, position, or in fact, any leverage at all, but I couldn't sit in my room until midnight while my friends were being tortured.

"I'll do it without you, you stupid snake-loving *veslingr*," I hissed as I hurried along the blood-colored corridors.

"You are not alone." Voror's voice entered my head, and to my surprise, tears sprang to my eyes. "I don't know if I can help you, but know you are not alone."

"Thank you, Voror. Do you know where they are?"

"No. But I am unable to enter the throne room through the walls. The magic protecting it is too strong."

"So you think they are in there?"

"I have not searched the whole palace, only the thrall quarters and the dungeons."

"Okay. Thank you."

"I do not understand how Orm knew this was happening," the owl said, and my pace faltered.

"You're right. He knew..."

"There is something between him and the Queen."

"Romantic?"

"Political."

I nodded. "Mazrith believes so too. They are planning something beyond these games."

I had reached the grand staircase and took the steps two at a time.

"Reyna, entering the Queen's throne room without the Prince is a dangerous thing to do."

"You think I don't know that?"

"You are armed with nothing but a wooden staff."

"Again, why are you telling me what I already know?"

"I am simply giving you a chance to re-evaluate your decision."

A fluttering of white caught my attention. He swooped down, landing on the wide balustrade just ahead of me. I stopped, and he blinked his huge eyes at me.

"I know, Voror. I know this is not a safe thing to do. But that's not going to stop me doing it. I have to know that my friends are not being harmed."

"And what will you do if they are?"

He was voicing the thought I was refusing to face.

What in the name of Odin *could* I do? The owl was right, I had nothing but a wooden staff. My only advantage over my enemies here was the shadow prince. The *absent* shadow prince.

"I'll think of something."

"The last time you thought of something, you offered yourself in their place. Reyna, you must not do that now."

I stared at him, throat constricting. "My life is not worth more than theirs."

"The fate of *Yggdrasil* rests upon you, Reyna. Do you remember that?"

"Of course I do," I muttered. Those stupid words swirled through my head, unbidden, regularly.

"You have a responsibility to your world."

"My world? They all fucking hate me! Treat me like shit! What do I owe this world?"

"You have seen but a fraction of the individuals that

5

make up *Yggdrasil*," Voror said sternly. "You presume to judge the entire world on a few rotten souls?"

I glared at him. "I want to see my friends."

"And I will be with you. But I will not allow you to make the wrong decision."

I was about to tell him that I couldn't see how he could stop me. I'd been making bad decisions my whole life, and so far, I was still standing, and so were my friends.

But the words didn't come.

Was the owl right? Was I judging a whole world on a few corrupt individuals?

And although I didn't believe my life to be worth more than anyone else's, I had accepted that I was a pawn in a game bigger than I was. It wasn't just Lhoris and Kara's lives depending on me now. Mazrith's was too.

And despite my anger with him, that meant something. More than I wanted or expected it to.

"Queen Andask!"

A male voice rang though the hallway, bouncing off the walls and laden with anger.

Voror took flight instantly, and Dakkar stormed into view at the bottom of the stairs.

His furious gaze caught mine, and he stilled. "Where is her throne room?"

I moved fast down the stairs as I pointed. "She took someone from you?"

"She will regret her twisted little games," he snarled.

All trace of the relaxed, confident fae I'd seen out in the games was gone.

Charged air whirled around his staff, flashing with

bright green, and his soft face was pinched and hard with anger.

I jogged to keep up with him, surprised to see the throne room doors open when we reached them.

My quick pace slowed instinctively when I reached the threshold of the horrible room, and I had to force my legs to keep moving, to carry me onto the long carpet that led to the Queen, sitting on her throne at the far end of the room. She was the only thing clearly lit; the rest of the room still shrouded in darkness. She wore an elaborate black fur collar adorned with red gems that caught the flickering candle-light, and my eyes went straight to the space above her head. Nothing was hanging above her this time, I was relieved to see.

Her lips curled up in a smile, revealing her black teeth, and she flicked the hand that held her staff.

The wall sconces all burst into flame, showing skull-filled urns lining the sides of the carpeted walkway, and a very tall curtain hanging on suspended beams on the left side of the throne. At another flick of her hand, the curtain dropped to the ground.

Dakkar gave a bark of anger. I raced forward.

Seven people and an exquisite golden crown were suspended in mid-air, ribbons of shadow wrapped around them.

They all looked to be asleep, but I barely took in any of their features. Lhoris and Kara were the last two in the row, and I moved straight to them.

"What have you done to them?" I demanded, at the same time Dakkar said almost the same words.

"They are unharmed," the Queen sang through a smile.

"You have no right!" the Earth fae shouted, moving down the carpet toward her throne.

"On the contrary, I have every right. The contract your Court signed on entering the *Leikmot* explicitly grants permission for an event just like this."

She pulled a piece of paper from somewhere beside her, and a slender tendril of shadow carried it to the fae.

His expression darkened, and she gave a tinkling laugh.

"Let me guess, Lord Dakkar. You can't read?" When he said nothing, she carried on speaking. "Well, you'll just have to take my word that the fine print containing the minutiae of our agreement makes this fair and honorable." She swung a hand toward the captives. "We must put on a show! This is the first time anything like this has been done in centuries. It would be a shame for it to be dull."

"There is something very wrong with you, your definition of honorable, and this whole accursed court," Dakkar hissed.

"Now, now. There is also much in the contract about good manners and respect for our brethren."

"Have you got into their heads?" My voice made both fae turn to me.

The Queen's eyes narrowed. "That, according the same contract, would be most untoward. Of course I haven't."

I didn't believe her, not for a second.

"If you have harmed one hair on my niece's head—" Dakkar started, and I felt a jolt of sympathy for the furious fae. But he didn't get to finish his sentence.

"Queen Andask! I congratulate you on such a shocking twist of events!"

Orm strode down the carpet, casting a cursory glance at the figures. I would bet everything I had that the crown was something precious to him. Interesting that he cared about at least one living being though. I scanned the figures, watching him too, trying to work out who his weak point might be.

"I had a feeling you would be impressed, Lord Orm," the Queen smiled at him.

Kaldar ran into the room before he could answer.

"Agda!" she called, then pulled up, taking in the scene around her. "What is the meaning of this?" She made it to the sleeping captives in a few long strides, pink tinging her pale cheeks.

"Ask Orm," I called, ensuring I got everyone's attention. "He knew about this."

The gold-fae put a hand to his chest, a defiant look on his face. "Of course I didn't. That is my own kin there," he said. He looked at the Queen. "You can assure all of us that they have not been harmed? The torture of innocents is prohibited in the contract." He shot a cruel glance at Dakkar. "I read every word carefully myself."

"They have been asleep the entire time they have been in my company," she smiled. "They will remain completely unharmed, lest you fail to win their safety at the ball this evening."

"That's not fair!"

"They never agreed to this. You can't use them like this!" I spoke at the same time as the other fae.

Orm said nothing.

The contract floated toward me, carried by the ribbon of shadow. "If you want to read this, or find someone who can for you, I swear you will find I am doing nothing wrong."

"I never agreed to any infernal contract!"

"You are the Shadow Court champion, little human. And the Shadow Court agreed."

"You will pay for this in kind, Andask," spat Kaldar, saving me from responding.

"I look forward to your inevitably insufficient attempt at revenge," the Queen said sweetly to her. "In the meantime, I swear by the power in my staff bestowed upon me by Odin, they shall come to no harm whatsoever between now and when you next see them at midnight."

"Well, there's no greater promise than that," Orm said with a shrug. He bowed low to her. "Until this evening," he said, then marched back down the carpet. Dakkar gave another bark of anger, then moved to the two brown-skinned fae hanging in the shadows. "I will be back," he whispered, then followed Orm out of the throne room. Kaldar gave a long look at her own folk, then left too.

I knew I should leave with them. Being alone with her was the last thing I should risk.

"You would not have taken them if Mazrith was here."

"I would, little girl. And besides, he is not here. So your musings are moot."

"I know what you're doing."

"No, you don't." She swiped her tongue across her lips slowly.

Soft footsteps sounded behind me and I saw Rangvald in

his long robes. "My Queen, there are preparations for tonight that require your attention." He turned to me. "Lady Frima requests you join her immediately in the Serpent Suites."

With a hiss, I turned to Lhoris and Kara. "Just hang on a few hours. And on Odin, I will kill her if she harms you."

2

REYNA

"Fucking Mazrith!" I kicked at the fireplace surround.

Brynja had worked on my hair and face to turn me into whatever the fuck I was supposed to look like to fit in with these maniacs.

When the maid had laid a host of dresses out in front of me, I instantly selected the one that stood out the most, a scarlet, boned bodice affair with a lightweight skirt and a long split that would allow me to move easily.

If all eyes were going to be on me and the other champions this evening, then I wanted to look bold. Confident. Send a message to the Queen who insisted on calling me 'little' at every opportunity.

But a dress wouldn't help me win my friends back.

What if I failed?

The thought had pervaded every infernal moment since I'd left the throne room.

What if the task set was too difficult, set for fae and not humans?

Of course it would be. The Queen was out to get me. Or at least to get to Mazrith, through me.

Anger with the Prince surged. "This would never have happened if he hadn't left!"

Frima shrugged, the loose straps of her black dress falling down her shoulder as she raised a glass of nettle wine to her lips. "Maybe not, but then the Starved Ones would have killed and eaten the human clans he has gone to protect. You'd prefer that?"

I glared at her. She was right, but I didn't need to be proven wrong right now. I needed to rage.

"He had a tantrum about me keeping secrets from him. How is that fair? I mean, would you tell somebody who had kidnapped you all your accursed secrets?"

She cocked her head at me. "What you two fight about is your own business. But Maz values honesty. For good reason."

"Well, I value my friends. And now, because of him, they might—" I screwed up my face, my words stalling abruptly.

Frima held out her glass to me. I bit my lip, then took it.

"Reyna, it is his fault you're all here, I grant you. But I think you know that this particular rage should be aimed at the Queen. Not at Maz. You need to channel it properly. Use it to show her up. To win."

"What..." I paused, then downed what was left in her glass, appreciating the burn. I stared at the empty vessel, my volume diminished to a whisper. "What if I can't?"

The fae woman took a deep breath, then clapped me

hard on the shoulder. "You will. You won that horserace. And, if it is a test designed for magic, then I'll do whatever I can to help you."

I snapped my eyes to hers. "You will?"

"When will you believe what is in front of you?" Her grip tightened on my bare shoulder. "I serve Maz. Until the end. And if he wants you safe, I want you safe." Her grip loosened. "And if he likes you, I do, too."

"I think... I think he *did* like me." My voice was still small.

"He'll come round."

I shook my head. "I saw something I shouldn't have. Something personal to him, and I never told him."

Frima's eyes sparked, and her lips tightened. "As much as I would love for you to tell me what is going on with him right now, you must stop. If he thinks you have shared his secrets, it will be worse."

"I wasn't going to tell you, I just..." I scrabbled for the right words. "I just need you to know that he's mad. Really mad."

"I recall you shouting too. Did he do something wrong? Other than, you know, kidnapping you."

"He snuck into my dreams," I scowled.

The corner of Frima's mouth quirked. "Fae wine dreams, per chance?"

My face flamed. "How did you know? Is that something he makes a habit of?" Anger flared.

She laughed. "No. But the way you two are with each other, it wasn't hard to guess. It's only a matter of time before you two kill each other or fuck each other."

I stepped back, unable to hold her laughing gaze. "Well, I don't think there's much chance of me killing him, what with him being an almighty fae and me being a human with stick."

"She's not human." Tait's words rang in my head, and I forced them out.

"Fair point. So, he kills you, or you fuck," she shrugged. "Was it a good dream?"

"I'm not answering that."

"That means yes." She moved to the drinks cabinet and got a fresh glass of wine.

"How long do we have until the ball?" I asked, desperate to change the subject, then immediately wishing I hadn't as the image of Lhoris and Kara hanging in the throne room filled my head.

"Long enough to drink this," she muttered, before looking at me. "You can do this Reyna. Without Maz."

Ellisar joined us as we made our way from the Serpent Suites to the feasting hall where the ball was to be held.

"How are you feeling?" I asked him.

"Thumping headache," he grunted. "Though at least everything isn't blue anymore. I did try to keep them safe," he added, giving me a sideways glance. It was the longest I'd ever seen the big man go without grinning.

"I believe you." In the same way Frima would do her master's bidding unto death, I was sure Ellisar would too. And unlike Svangrior, I had a feeling he resented us less.

"If the Queen has caused them any harm, I'll ensure I'm dealt the same amount of pain. It is my fault she has them."

My eyebrows rose at his words. Valor. Honor. Loyalty. They were the *Yggdrasil* values so absent from the Gold Court.

"She swore she would not cause them harm."

He nodded. "I pray she has kept her word, and that your task suits you."

"Chess, then," I muttered.

"It could be," said Frima. We had reached the grand staircase, and I could see fae moving across the bold tiles below, bedecked in their finery.

"We can but hope."

When we reached the open doors to the feast hall, my breath caught, and I felt Frima tense beside me.

"Blessed Odin," she breathed.

"She's not fucking around," muttered Ellisar.

He wasn't wrong. The Queen had made certain her guests would never forget their visit to the Shadow Court palace.

The urns I had seen before in the throne room now lined the maroon walls in the massive hall, filled to bursting with skulls. The cavernous ceiling was strung with black and silver ribbons long enough to almost reach the guests, which would have looked pretty if they weren't once again adorned with eyeballs. A giant horseshoe-shaped table dominated the room, laden with platters of food, and hundreds of fae dressed in the finest clothes I'd ever seen were standing in groups, drinking and talking in the space between the table.

The floor was what drew my eye, though. It was made of glass, and below it, flowing quickly and catching the light, appeared to be a twisting, turning, river of blood.

"Please tell me that's a trick or glamor, and this palace doesn't actually have rivers of blood running under the rooms," I whispered, pointing.

Frima didn't reply.

A thrall dressed in fine black robes banged a small drum beside the door as we took a step into the room.

"Presenting Prince Mazrith Andask's betrothed, Reyna Thorvald."

The entire room fell quiet, more than a hundred heads turning our way. I straightened my back, and willed the powders Brynja had applied to hide the color I knew would be rushing my face.

Another well-dressed thrall rushed over, handing us glasses of wine.

Frima moved, and I forced my legs to move with her, into the room. Every fae we passed offered tense words of congratulations, badly veiled suspicion and distaste on every pair of lips.

Standing over the fast-flowing river below made me nervous, my eyes constantly drawn to the movement. It didn't look far to fall, but after my recent encounter in the shrine I had no desire to stand on a see-through floor.

All I wanted to do was get my friends back.

I scanned the crowd for the Queen, spotting her at the head of the horseshoe table. After another few minutes of smiling and nodding at fae who would plunge a dagger into my chest as soon as they would speak to me, I made my way to her.

She was wearing black and green, a magnificent dress set off by even more magnificent jewelry. I tried to look at her staff, but it shimmered out of focus every time I locked my gaze on it.

"Reyna. You almost look like you belong here," she said to me in her sickly-sweet tone.

"You look charming," Rangvald said with a small bow of his head.

Before I had a chance to reply, she banged her staff on the glass floor.

My pulse rocketed.

"Guests! Our champions have all arrived. Let the entertainment begin!"

The space between the tables clouded over with shadow, and when it dissipated, there was a long beam high above the room.

Each of the captives were tied around the middle with a rope, which had then been thrown over the beam, and secured in a large black box on a pedestal on the other side.

They looked as though they were still sleeping, albeit ten feet off the floor.

"Champions, move to the boxes holding your loved ones, if you will," the Queen called with a smile.

We all did as she asked.

"The rope holding them is tied inside the boxes. All you need do is untie them. Although I recommend having someone to catch them. It is a bit of a fall," she added with a tinkling laugh.

I looked at the two boxes. They had no lid or hinges, just a round hole in the front, filled with dark, opaque shadows.

What was in there?

"To add an element of excitement to the proceedings, let me introduce some pets of mine," the Queen said.

She waved her hand, and eight enormous spiders appeared on the beam, one above each hanging captive. As if held back by some invisible force, their legs swished, but the spiders didn't move.

I bit down hard on my tongue, my insides turning to mush.

All spiders in *Yggdrasil* were venomous.

"Whilst they are fairly slow, their venom is incredibly potent," she sang. "So please, if you value your loved ones' lives, do not dally."

A drum banged somewhere, and the crowd gave a surge of whispered excitement.

"Go!"

Whatever was holding the spiders back vanished, and I plunged my hand into the box holding Kara.

3

REYNA

Water, was my first thought.

Pain was my second.

Shocks zinged up from a hundred places on my hand, shooting up my arm and fizzing out when they reached my shoulder.

I gritted my teeth and heard a curse from Orm next to me.

Satisfaction at the fae experiencing pain forced me on. As I moved my hand through the water, searching for the rope holding Kara up, I felt hundreds of soft slithery things moving against my skin, accompanying the constant shocks. Electric eels.

I balled my hand into a fist, trying to give my palm a second's relief, then kept searching, doing all I could to ignore the shocks.

With a jolt of relief, my fingers closed around a peg with

a coarse rope attached firmly to it. Finding the part where the knot was tightest, I began to pull at the cord.

The shocks changed as soon as I did, the intensity ramping up from painful to outright agony.

I heard more curses from both sides of me and assumed the others had found the rope too. Closing my eyes, I took a deep breath and concentrated, forcing my fingers to work through the pain. But the shocks and the cold water were having a second effect, and that was a numbing of my fingers that was becoming hard to ignore.

"Come on, Reyna," I hissed to myself. The rope was coming loose at the widest point, and I traced my fingers along the rest of it, working out where to pull next.

There was a hiss from the crowd, and my eyes opened, my gaze going straight to the spiders. They were making their way along the rope, fast, though none had yet begun their descent toward their prey.

I redoubled my efforts, giving an involuntary cry as the rope abruptly gave way under my almost lifeless fingers' tugging.

"Frima!" I yelled as the rope went slack then Kara's body began to fall toward the ground.

Frima darted forward from the crowd, just catching Kara. Another body began to fall, a blue-haired fae running forward to catch them.

I looked back to the boxes, wasting no time before pushing my other, less-numb, hand into the next box.

The pain this time was instantly excruciating. Instinct took over completely, my hand flying back out of the box, whatever had bitten me still attached.

I stared dazedly down at the sickly yellow scorpion attached to the bottom of my thumb, before my senses kicked back in. I slammed my hand toward the ground, dislodging it. It scuttled off and I sucked in a breath as the wound on my hand began turning green. I didn't know how many more were in there, but I did know that Lhoris's life was dependent on me.

"It's just pain, Reyna," I said through gritted teeth.

"It will be over fast," Voror's voice sounded in my head.

"Thank you, Voror," I whispered, and plunged my hand back in.

There were at least five more in there, I thought, tears streaming from my eyes as they stabbed their stingers into my flesh over and over.

I was quicker finding the rope this time, but the pain was making me unable to work my fingers properly, all my senses blurring into one hot, agonizing mass.

I fumbled at the rope, aware that I'd made a lot less progress than I had on Kara's rope by this point, but refusing to look at the spider moving toward Lhoris.

With a vicious curse, I pulled my hand out quickly, hoping to dislodge more of the evil creatures.

Two came out with me and I flicked them off hard. I blinked at my hand. It was so swollen I was amazed my fingers had done anything at all to the rope. I shoved my other hand in, blessedly able to feel the rope properly. I tugged at the cord as hard as I could, before the stinging started anew.

The crowd cheered and I couldn't help looking. Orm's crown fell to the floor.

Without me wanting them to, my eyes darted to Lhoris' rope. The spider was a foot from his helpless body.

I pulled at the rope, but it hadn't loosened at all. My pulse raced so fast I was getting dizzy, and I tried to suck in air as I forced my fingers to their mark.

A slow beat started as the guests drummed their fingers on the tables and tapped their feet in a crescendo. *A countdown.*

They thought this was entertainment? A fucking game for their viewing pleasure?

"This is barbaric!" Dakkar's furious voice shouted.

I heard Kaldar give a strangled cry.

Fury was washing out the pain, but my stupid hand wouldn't work. I looked down at the other one, wondering if I could swap again, but if anything, it had swollen up more.

"Come on, you Odin-cursed bastard," I pulled as hard as I could at the rope, but my fat fingers couldn't even grip it anymore.

A sense of dread coiled through me as I realized that both my hands were now useless.

I couldn't do it. I couldn't untie the rope before the spider reached him.

"Frima!" I called, looking past the hanging captives at the fae woman.

Her face was impassive, but her eyes were filled with anger. Her grip on her staff tightened even as my grip on the rope slipped away entirely.

Would she help him? Go against the queen and the rules of the game to save a gold-giver she didn't know?

Please, please, please, Freya, Odin, and *Frima*, please save him.

Shadows erupted across the room, a huge bang drawing everybody's attention.

Everybody's except mine.

My eyes were glued to the ropes. The shadows sliced through them like they were butter. Lhoris fell hard, Frima only just noticing in time and catching most of his weight, stopping his head hitting the hard floor. Kaldar's captive landed hard on the fae beneath her, who was staring at the door.

I pulled my hand from the box, tears blurring my vision. I turned to the doors.

I already knew who I would see.

Mazrith filled the archway. Shadows swirled around him in a cloud of fury, his skull mask glinting menacingly. His huge shoulders were bare, and his chest was lathered in black war paint. His black, braided hair hung loose over his shoulders.

I sank to my knees as his eyes found mine.

Thank you. Thank you. Thank you.

I knew he couldn't hear my thoughts. But I sent them anyway. I projected them in every way I could.

"You would use my absence to play games with our guests?" Mazrith growled as he stepped into the room.

A flash of an unnatural sound, and a sense of something very wrong washed over me. I glanced at my hands.

The scorpion venom playing with my mind?

"Nothing you wouldn't have done yourself, my son." The

Queen smiled as everyone parted, leaving a route between the two royals.

"On the contrary. I have been defending our Court, and our guests, from an unprecedented attack."

"Unprecedented?" The repeated use of her own word was lost on nobody. "I doubt that, dear son," she smiled.

"Oh, believe me, stepmother. This is truly unprecedented."

He raised his staff and six warriors moved into the room from behind him. They were carrying a cage between them, shadows swirling around the bars. They didn't hide what was in it though.

I tipped backward, my legs unable to hold my weight, even on my knees.

It was a Starved One.

4

REYNA

The Queen opened her mouth, then closed it again. I stared between them, doing whatever I could not to look at the Starved One thrashing about in the cage, its hideous groans ringing through the shocked silence in the feast hall.

The Queen cast a glance at Orm, who stepped away from the boxes. His captive was coming around, blinking and murmuring into the quiet.

"Prince Mazrith," Orm said, spreading his arms wide. "Is this really appropriate to bring to a party?"

Mazrith snarled at him. "What is inappropriate is having a party while our Court is attacked by monsters! Where is the chief of the royal guard?" He whirled on the Queen. She glanced at Rangvald with a nod, and he hurried off, giving Mazrith and the cage a wide berth.

Kaldar moved quickly, straight to two young, unconscious blue-haired fae.

"My apologies to our guests for this interruption," the Queen said loudly.

Dakkar spoke, ignoring the Queen entirely and directing his words at Mazrith. "They attacked your Court?"

"Yes. We drove them back beyond the root-river."

"Were the casualties high?" The unspoken part of that question hung heavy in the air. *Were they able to create many more Starved Ones from the humans they slaughtered?*

"We got there in time to limit the damage." Mazrith's answer was brusque. "This party is adjourned. There will be a war council at dawn." He glanced between Kaldar, Dakkar and Orm. "As you find yourselves part of this, you may join if you wish."

He banged his staff on the ground, and the six warriors lifted the cage and backed out of the room. Svangrior strode into the room and headed straight for Frima and my friends. Lhoris was waking up, his face pale and his eyes dilated. Kara was still asleep. Svangrior bent and scooped the girl up. Frima helped pull Lhoris to his feet, mumbling something about explaining everything soon.

My head still spinning but my pulse finally slowing, I tried to get to my feet. My hands roared with pain, so swollen now it looked like I was wearing a huge pair of sickly green gloves.

Cold touched my sides, then something was aiding my movements.

Shadows. They swirled around me, helping me to stand. I locked eyes with Mazrith. He hadn't moved. I kept my sight on him, not looking at the Queen or the streams of chattering fae on either side of me as I moved toward the doors.

"Thank you," I said, when I reached the hulking fae Prince. "He would have died."

Fury danced in his pale eyes behind the mask. "To the Serpent Suites. Now."

As soon as we were in the Prince's rooms, everyone spoke at once.

"Is she... is she okay?" Ellisar's voice was uncharacteristically quiet as Svangrior set Kara down in the armchair.

"She'll be fine," the fae warrior muttered. Lhoris moved to her side as I did. She looked peaceful, her chest rising and falling steadily.

"What happened?" Lhoris asked, looking at me as the fae all directed questions at Mazrith.

"The Queen took you both. To play a game with the champions," I started to tell him, but Mazrith's voice boomed over everyone's, cutting us all off.

"Reyna. Come with me."

He marched into his bedroom, and I gulped back my trepidation and followed him.

"I meant what I said. Thank you for saving Lhoris," I started as soon as I entered the room. It was dark inside, the fire low.

Mazrith removed his mask, pushing his hair back from his face. The beads in his braids glinted in the firelight, his eyes flashing as he looked at me.

"Washroom."

I raised my eyebrows.

"Have they stopped hurting?" He pointed at my hands.

I realized with a jolt that they had. "Yes."

"Then you don't have much time before you start losing fingertips. Washroom."

I hurried after him, into the more brightly lit bathing chamber. He pointed at the copper bathtub, and I perched on the side of it and held out both my hands.

Shadows swirled from his staff, wrapping around my swollen hands.

Mazrith stayed silent.

"What are the shadows doing?" I asked. It was hard to sound casual, but I tried.

"Those scorpions are of this court, and of shadow magic. I can draw out the venom. The wounds from the punctures will heal normally," he answered, his voice clipped. He was watching the shadows, not my face.

"Mazrith." Slowly, his eyes met mine. "I didn't tell you about the vision I had of your mother because I guess I didn't truly trust you. But now... I do."

You are a liar and a hypocrite. I am done with you.

His words rang through my mind as he stared at me. Silently.

My stomach tightened. "If you're healing me, you must be at least a little less angry?"

"I do not want you dead."

"Well, that's something I suppose." I gave him an awkward smile, which he didn't return. I sighed. "Look, I get it, you don't like being lied to."

"It is more than that, and you know it," he growled. "You

claim terror at your secrets being drawn from your mind, and yet you were..." He trailed off, glaring.

I squared my shoulders, mentally preparing myself. "There's a reason I'm scared of my secrets being discovered," I said slowly.

"Because you are not human?" His words were a snarl.

I narrowed my eyes. "Of course I'm human. I don't know what's happening to me, but I can guarantee you, I am human."

He grunted.

I swallowed again, harder. "No, a different reason. I have more to tell you. Not about you, about me. But only if you'll still work with me to get to the bottom of all of this."

Shadows danced through his bright eyes as he stared into mine. I forced myself to hold his probing gaze.

"Tell me exactly what you saw. Of me, and my mother."

I nodded. "I'll tell you everything. If you see this through with me."

"I will not be blackmailed, gildi." He bared his teeth as he spoke, leaning forward from the wall. "Tell me what you know of me, what you kept from me, and I will decide where we go from here."

I closed my eyes, took a breath, and told him exactly what I had seen in the vision of his mother, and then in the second vision with the mist-staff.

When I opened them again, he was no longer looking at me, but at the tiled floor. "That is everything?"

"About you, yes." His eyes moved back to mine and I shifted uncomfortably. If I was going to be completely

COURT OF MONSTERS AND MALICE

honest with him, then I should probably do it right. "Except, erm, one other thing that is a bit more recent."

Anger crossed his features. I tried to hold up my hands in innocent protest but the shadows held them in place. "It happened after our fight!"

"What did?"

"Well, this is the other thing I need to tell you. And I'm only going to do that if we're going to go back to helping each other."

He sighed. A long, growly sigh.

"I do not trust you."

A flicker of annoyance took me. "Hey, this is a two-way thing, you know. You've hardly been innocent in all this trust horseshit. Not only did you kidnap me and threaten to kill my friends, which is hardly the basis for a healthy exchange of trust, you snuck into my private thoughts after promising not to!"

His look softened a touch. "I am sorry for that."

"You are?"

"For betraying your trust, yes. Not for getting what I needed through a dream instead of from your bed. Nor for taking you from the Gold Court."

My cheeks warmed. A pleasant tingling was running through my wrists and into my fingers, and I tried to concentrate on that.

"Yes, well. This would be more complicated if we had, erm, you know."

Mazrith said nothing.

I chewed the inside of my lip for a moment, then looked

down at my hands. The green swelling was mostly gone, red puncture wounds covering the skin instead.

"I am sorry, too," I said quietly. "That I didn't tell you sooner. And that you lost your mom."

He didn't reply for a while. "How many times in your life have you used that word?"

I looked up at him. "Sorry?" He nodded. "Not many. Does that help?"

"Yes."

"So, you forgive me?"

"No. And I still do not trust you." He took a deep breath, and I noticed the shallow, fresh cuts along his shoulders. "But we will see this through. I believe the fates have left us no choice."

I scowled at him. "If I'm going to bare all my secrets, I'm going to need more than that."

He shrugged, and his hair fell over his shoulders. "That's all I am giving you."

"So even if I tell you everything I've got, you won't tell me about your curse, or your mother?"

"I will tell you nothing more than you need to know. Just as before." He pushed himself off the wall, moving quickly and dropping into a crouch before me, our eyes level. He reached out a hand, using his thumb and finger to hold my chin still. My heart thudded in my chest, my breathing tight as his gaze pinned me as firmly as he had physically.

When he spoke his voice was low. "This is not about me, little liar. This, I am beginning to believe, is about you. Which means you tell me everything, and we work out what the fates *you* are supposed to do to fix this fucking mess."

5

REYNA

"It's the middle of the night," I said, staring at Mazrith tear into a leg of chicken. "Can't we talk about this tomorrow?"

"No," he said without looking at me. We were in two chairs in front of the now-reinvigorated fireplace in his bedroom. A trolley covered in food was before him, and I guessed battling Starved Ones had taken its toll because I fully believed he would devour the lot.

"I eat, you talk," he said. "Then I hold the War Council and work out how to stop the humans of my Court becoming undead by the end of the week."

I shifted in my seat and took a sip of the drink he had given me. My tastebuds lit up. Coffee.

"Okay. So, I guess there are two main things. But they both involve visions."

He said nothing, just kept eating.

I took another sip of my drink and decided to start with

the easier admission. "During the rock-throwing challenge, something happened. At the time, I thought it might have been you or Frima helping me. But now, I'm not so sure, because it happened again during the last game, and neither of you were close enough to have caused it."

He paused with some bread halfway to his mouth and looked at me. "The last game," he said quietly, as though he had completely forgotten about it.

I nodded. "It went well."

"It did? Idunn did well?"

"Idunn did nothing. Your stepmother assigned us all horses and she gave me Rasa."

Mazrith froze. "My mother's horse?"

"Yep."

His eyes raked quickly over me. "I am amazed you do not have broken limbs."

I gave him a look that I hoped wasn't as smug as I felt. "She happens to like me," I said. "I think we share a desire for freedom."

His face softened completely, a warm expression I wasn't sure I'd ever seen on him before. "She raced well?"

"Incredibly. We won."

Light flared in his eyes, replaced quickly by shadow. "I am pleased to hear that."

"You and me both. But, let me tell you what helped me win. Apart from Rasa, of course. During both the rock throwing and the race, visions came to me."

"Like the one of my mother?" His voice was guarded again, the warmth gone.

"No. Nothing like those. I was seeing through my opponent's eyes, in real-time. And getting a sense of their feelings. Hate or glee, or fear."

The Prince lowered his hand, dropping bread on the trolley. "And you thought it was one of us?"

"Yes. Helping me. You have mind magic."

He shook his head. "The Queen is the only one who could do that, with the power of a mist-staff."

I swallowed. "I've had one other vision like that."

His gaze bore into me.

"Through, erm, your eyes. You were talking to Tait. And he told you I wasn't human."

"So now you are a spy," Mazrith growled.

"Not intentionally! I have no control over it. It only started after you brought me here."

After an uncomfortable pause he spoke again. "And the second thing you need to tell me?"

I took a bigger sip of my drink. "Lhoris started to take care of me when I was about ten, we think. And I have no memory of my life before then. But one thing I do know is that whenever I work with gold, I experience intense visions afterward." I couldn't look at him as I spoke. The only person I had ever told this to was Lhoris, more than a decade ago.

My whole life I had known, as certainly as I'd known anything, that I had to keep my visions a secret. It was wrong for others to know, wrong on a bone-deep level.

I closed my eyes, forcing myself to carry on. This was bigger than me now. I couldn't get to the end on my own. Which meant I had to share.

"The vision is always the same. Well, it was, until the

one I saw your mother in. There are three, sometimes four waves of them. And I hear, smell, then see the same thing."

"What do you see?" His question hung heavy in the air, and I felt sick. I forced my lips apart, then answered him.

"The Starved Ones."

Silence swamped the room.

Eventually, he spoke. "You've had visions of the Starved Ones your entire life." It wasn't a question, more of a disbelieving statement.

"Yes."

"And you honestly believe that you are human?"

I made myself look at him. "I *am* human. Rune-marked, but human."

"I can't decide whether to believe you or not."

"About the visions?"

"No, about whether you really believe you are human."

I glared at him. "Why would I lie?"

"Because you are a liar."

I stood up, barely restraining myself from kicking at the chair in annoyance. "I just told you something I have never told anyone, and you're calling me a liar and insulting me? If that's how you're going to be, then I'm done talking with you. I'm too tired for this shit."

"I'm sorry."

His words took the wind from my sails. I couldn't see any sorrow in his face, but he'd said the words, immediately. "Really?"

"For upsetting you? Yes. Really. Sit down."

I did, rubbing my hand over my face and flinching at the many sting wounds. It had been a long day, and I was tired.

Bone-deep exhaustion fueled by relief that my friends were now safe was mixing with the adrenaline caused by divulging my greatest secret to the fae prince.

Mazrith was still staring at me, his expression thoughtful, not fearful.

Not that I hadn't expected him to fear me, but judge me? Be disgusted by me perhaps? Nobody should have any kind of connection to those creatures.

Taking courage, I looked into his eyes and gave voice to the fear I had carried alone my whole life. "They know who I am. I've seen them my whole life, and now I'm wondering if they have been trying to communicate with me all that time. What if I mean something to them?"

Mazrith held my gaze.

"They have never converged on a Court before like they have here, or tried to block the root-river. I do believe it is you they are after. And clearly, the reason goes back further than our current quest."

My stomach tightened and bile rose in my throat as the Elder's voice sang through my mind. They had nearly got me, that night. And now they had gotten bold enough to attack the Court I was in.

"Why could they want me? What could I possibly have that they could want?"

The Prince's eyes darkened as they pierced mine. "I do not know. Is there anything else at all you need to tell me?"

The words of Voror's mysterious fae washed through my mind. *The fate of Yggdrasil.*

But as I opened my mouth to speak, Voror's voice entered my mind. "Do not tell him about the fae who visited me," he said. "She was very clear that her existence must be revealed to nobody but you."

I did my best to keep my face clear, but Mazrith must have seen my expression change. He gave me a questioning look, then cast his eyes upward. "Your owl speaks to you?"

"Yes."

Mazrith quirked an eyebrow. "And? He bids you keep secrets from me?"

I nodded slowly. "They are not mine to share, but his."

Mazrith thought for a minute. "That is fair. His secrets are not yours. But I must trust you to tell me anything you think is important."

I chewed my tongue, thinking. "He believes my fate is connected to more than just yours," I said, hoping that was vague but impactful enough.

Mazrith nodded. "I'm inclined to agree."

He went back to eating, and I forced my muscles to relax, to sink into the squishy chair. I had done it. I had told him my secret, and nothing terrible had happened. I hadn't exploded into flames, Mazrith had not banished me from his Court or handed me to the monsters. He had just gone back to eating chicken.

We sat in silence for a while, probably an hour, and I was dozing in my chair when his voice reached me.

"We must visit the Starved One."

"What?" I mumbled.

"The Starved One I brought here as captive. We must visit it."

I blinked, sitting up and staring at him. "No."

"I want to see what it does when it sees you."

My mouth fell open, my drowsiness expelled. "We don't need to visit it to know the answer to that - it will try to eat me! That's what they all do!"

He stood up. "Reyna, we need to find out what your connection to them is. This is an opportunity."

"No! Why did you even bring it here?"

He dropped my gaze. "To prove to the other fae that the threat was real. But now, we must take advantage and gain information from it."

A shudder took me. "It's not an Elder, is it?" It hadn't spoken in the cage in the feast hall. "They can't speak."

"I do not need words to get information," he said quietly.

My skin crawled. "You want to get into its head?" I whispered.

"Yes." He looked back at me. "And if I can do so while you're there, maybe I can find out what you mean to them."

6

MAZRITH

Reyna didn't speak a word as she followed me to the cells. I didn't even think she was trying to remember or keep track of the path we were taking through the palace to the spire that held captives of the Shadow Court. Well, the captives my stepmother wasn't keeping for her fucked-up pleasure.

When we reached the guarded entrance, her fear was palpable, and she was doing everything she could to hide it. But the tremble in her legs and the darting of her eyes gave her away.

I knew I couldn't trust her. Knew she would likely be the death of me. But I hated seeing her scared.

It was necessary, though. As were too many things I hated.

I needed to know why they wanted her. I needed to know what the true risk to my people was, how far they would go to get her.

And I needed to know what the risk to Reyna was.

The noise the creature was making almost made her steps falter as we moved through the cold, stone corridors. A gurgling sound, as though its throat had been cut and it couldn't breathe properly. Which, given that it was undead, was entirely possible.

Human prisoners cowered in the corners of their cells, and a twinge of regret that they must listen to the creature's gurgled wails almost made me stop - until I remembered that they were all in here for breaking the laws of the Court. The real laws, not the Queen's horseshit. Every resident of these cells was a danger to others' safety.

As soon as we rounded the corner to the cell containing the Starved One, it locked its one-eyed gaze on Reyna. It flew off the ground on two mismatched legs, launching itself at the bars. The wet gurgling got louder, and it clawed its rotten arms between the metal to reach her, the little flesh it had catching on the rough bars, exposed bone clattering.

Reyna breathed hard but held her ground, as far away as the small space would allow her to be.

"Good," I told her quietly. "You are safe."

She didn't look at me, her wide eyes locked on the frenzied creature.

"Just do what you need to do so I can get the fuck out of here," she said through clenched teeth.

I channeled my thoughts into my staff, and shadows whirled from it, flowing toward the creature. It stilled a moment, having seen enough of its brethren torn apart by the ribbons of black to be wary of them.

The tendrils wrapped around the thing's head, and I had to concentrate on not recoiling.

Death, rotten flesh, despair, and most of all, *hunger*.

Hunger like I had never experienced - never even known it was possible to experience. All-encompassing, all consuming, hunger. There was not enough food in the world to sate this creature.

I began to probe, forcing my reluctant power further into the creature's mind.

"Step forward," I said quietly to Reyna. She drew a breath, then obliged.

The thing swiped for her, a strong sensation bursting through the hunger.

Salvation.

I frowned. From the hunger? Was her flesh any different from any others?

Yes... It believed that she could provide satisfaction. Fullness. She was different.

"Have you got what you need?" Reyna's voice was tight, and I released my shadows.

I would not put her through anymore.

"Yes."

"Thank Freya, let's—" But she didn't finish her sentence. She swayed on her feet a moment, her eyes glazing over.

I swore, moving to steady her. Her skin was clammy and cold, and she gasped. There was a second of clarity in her expression before her eyes unfocused again.

There were three or four waves of the visions, she had told me.

A bead of sweat rolled down her temple, and her hands shook.

I had caused this. She hadn't wanted to come here, and I had forced her.

Making sure I didn't channel my anger into the grip I had on her arm, I watched as the third wave took her, her chest heaving with hard breaths.

The Starved One screeched and rattled behind the bars, and I considered bodily lifting her off her feet and carrying her from the dungeons.

Her eyes cleared before I could though, focusing on me. "Please, can we leave, now?"

"You are capable of walking?"

"To get out of here, I'd make myself capable of fucking flying," she rasped.

We left the dungeons quickly, the color returning to her cheeks as soon as we were out of earshot of the Starved One. She didn't speak until we had reached the Serpent Suites though. The sitting room was empty, and she moved immediately to the drinks cabinet.

"What did you find out from its thoughts?"

"It wants you. It believes you're different. That you can end its hunger."

Her hands shook as she poured what looked like the nettle wine that Frima loved into a glass.

"Why?"

"I don't think it has the capacity to understand why. Even as a concept."

Disappointment painted her features as she snapped her head to me. "So that was for nothing."

"No. It confirms that they are here for you."

She looked away. "We already knew that," she said quietly.

"What did you see in the vision?" I asked. "The Elder again?"

She didn't answer me for a moment. "Yes. But she didn't speak to me. And the background was different." She took a long sip from her drink. "It's usually a cave or something, and I can see what I always guessed were more Starved Ones moving around. But this time there were people fighting outside. It was blurry. But I saw someone tied to a tree. I think they set fire to them. The Elder watched, then turned to me and laughed." Reyna shuddered, then emptied the glass, her eyes closing. "I don't understand how I can have anything to do with them. With anything so..."

She didn't finish the sentence. She wouldn't admit to her terror aloud, in front of me.

If these creatures had invaded her mind her whole life... Her fear of mind magic made sense. The terror I had caused in her after the snake attack made sense.

Every instinct in me had me stepping across the room toward her.

I opened my mouth, ready to tell her that I knew fear that deep.

That I respected her for facing it, when others would not.

That I would never let her fear anything again if I could help it.

Just in time, I clamped my mouth shut, and drew on everything I had to still my feet.

I knew what would happen if I comforted her. If I relented in my anger and distrust so fast.

I needed that anger, needed that distrust, to keep us far enough apart to fulfill the plan fate had for us.

"Get some sleep. It is almost day, and I must attend the War Council."

7

REYNA

I .was drawn from my fitful sleep by a gentle hand on my cheek. I jerked awake, groping for the intruder's wrist, then cursing as my wounded fingers made contact.

"Reyna, it's me."

"Kara." The girl came into bleary view as I blinked. "Thank Freya you're okay."

She tipped forward, hugging me into the pillows. "Thanks to you, I hear."

"Thanks to Mazrith, actually." She refused to let go, so I stayed where I was, laying in the bed, her small body pressed to my side.

"Reyna?" she whispered.

"Yes?"

"Don't tell Lhoris, but I don't think these fae are the villains."

"I'm glad to hear that, because I think I agree with you," I whispered back, squeezing her tighter.

She lifted my arm, and peered at my hand. "These look sore."

"They are. But they were worse yesterday. Maz removed the scorpion venom."

"Maz?"

"Yeah, the big bad fae who took us captive?"

She giggled. "I know who he is. I've just not heard you call him *Maz* before."

I frowned. She was right. I hadn't called him that before. "Hmm. Well, I've decided to trust him."

"That's probably wise."

It had taken me a while, despite my fatigue, to sleep after the visit to the cells and the Starved One. Hours had passed where I knew I couldn't sleep, or I would be drawn instantly into the nightmares. Once the adrenaline caused by seeing, and hearing, the creature up close and the startling new vision had passed, my thoughts had shifted firmly back to Mazrith and my relief that he had gotten over his anger and that I was no longer hiding anything from him was stronger than I had imagined it would be.

"Kara, I want to tell you something." I sat up, dislodging her. She sat up too, pulling a fur blanket around her shoulders.

"My bed isn't this nice," she said.

"This is the Prince's bed. It's likely the nicest in the Court."

"Other than his crazy stepmom's."

"I shudder to think what her bed looks like. Anyway,

listen. Last night I told the Prince some stuff about myself that only Lhoris knows. And I want you to know too."

"But what if the Queen-" I held my hand up.

"I thought about that. If Lhoris knows, then she'll get the information anyway. Maybe already has."

Kara shook her head. "Only if she did it while we were asleep. Neither of us remembers anything."

"Well, hopefully she is telling the truth and stayed out of your heads. Either way though, I want you to know this about me. You're more than just my friend, you're my family, and it feels wrong you not knowing."

There was a flap of wings from high in the ceiling beams. "Come on down, Voror. I guess I owe you an explanation too."

"I was present when you told the Prince, but I will listen again before offering my extremely valuable opinion."

"You're too kind."

I told Kara everything. It was easier, the second time, though the words hardly flowed effortlessly. I didn't know if Kara would take it as well as the war-worn shadow-fae Prince, but to my relief, she didn't run screaming when I was done. Instead, she stared wide-eyed at me.

"Reyna, he's right, you can't be human." she said eventually.

I scowled at her. "Don't be ridiculous. How could I be anything else?"

"You don't know who your parents are."

"Look at me. I'm as human as you are."

She shook her head emphatically. "I don't have visions

of monsters or see through other people's eyes. That's magic."

"It is magic, I agree, but it must be coming from someone or something else."

I looked at the owl for backup. "I am less convinced of my original theory," he said.

"What? Why?"

"I did not know then that you had experienced visions since childhood."

"Those visions are different."

He fluttered his wings. "Mind magic is mind magic."

"Mind magic?" I stared at him.

"What is he saying?" Kara asked, and I filled her in. "I think he's right, it definitely sounds like mind magic to me," she said.

"But only shadow-fae have that, and I'm quite clearly not a shadow-fae." I thrust my wrist out. "Look, I have a gold rune-mark. That *only human gold-givers* can have."

They both looked at the mark, then at the black one next to it.

"Could the Prince's mark have given you magic?" Kara asked doubtfully.

"I think he would have mentioned that last night. But maybe I'll ask him."

Voror hooted softly. "You have had visions of monsters since your youth. The mark has nothing to do with it."

I sighed and told Kara what he'd said.

"The mark might be causing the spying visions, if those only started since you got here?" she suggested.

I screwed up my nose at the word *spying* but didn't say

anything. It was the most accurate way to differentiate them from the other visions. *Could* Mazrith have passed magic into me with the mark?

"So, just to get it straight, the spying visions have helped you?"

"Yes. I don't think I would have won the last game without them. Although Rasa *was* amazing." A massive desire to visit the horse took me, and I swung my legs out of bed.

"Then maybe they are being sent by a magical ally, and nothing to do with the other ones." She beamed at me suddenly. "I'm so happy you won. I wish I could have seen you beating that awful gold-fae Lord to the finish line. Does that mean you'll get your braid?"

I paused in gathering trousers, a black shirt and my leather wrap from the wardrobe. "In all the confusion, I hadn't really thought..."

A knock sounded at the door, then it was pushed open. Frima put her head round. "Mazrith wants you for whatever your secret stuff is, as soon as you're ready."

I nodded at her, remembering the jade that was hidden in my dresser. We had a statue to fix.

When the door was closed again, Kara climbed off the bed and came over to me. "I think everything that is happening to you is connected. And whatever you are doing with the Prince will hopefully lead to answers."

I bit my cheek. "What about the Starved Ones?"

"Mazrith won't let them get you," she said confidently.

"I mean, why do I have a connection to them? What if

that has nothing to do with the things that have only happened since we came here, to the Shadow Court?"

She gave me a small smile. "The Prince came for you. The Starved Ones want you." She pointed at Voror. "A magical owl found you. The fates will give you answers Reyna. Just stay alive long enough to find them."

I leaned in to hug her.

She was right. I couldn't let the Starved Ones, the Queen, Lord Orm — any of them — rattle me. As long as Mazrith and I got the mist-staff, we could at least remove his curse and hopefully the twisted Queen from power. Perhaps that would be the thing that changed the fate of *Yggdrasil*, the thing I was destined to be a part of. Restoring the Shadow Court to an honorable leader might have a massive impact on the world.

"How can someone so young be so wise?" I muttered into Kara's hair.

She squeezed me back. "The same way you're so strong," she whispered back.

8

REYNA

I was forced to draw on Kara's faith in my strength
when Mazrith and I reached the statue under the
mountain an hour later. She didn't know about my
newfound trouble with heights — unlike the prince.

He offered me his hand as soon as he had climbed out of
the boat, and unlike before, I took it. I sat straight down on
the stone to prevent my legs from shaking, and then shuf-
fled across the stone before him on my backside.

The shame I had felt last time wasn't gripping me, and I
wasn't sure if that was because Mazrith already knew that I
was no longer able to walk across the bridge out over the
chasm, or because I was actually less ashamed of my fear.

Once we had reached the outstretched hand, I got carefully to my feet and Voror swooped down, landing on the
stone head of one of the faceless statues.

I moved cautiously to the shadow-fae statue, Mazrith's
hulking form right behind me. "Here goes." I fished the jade

from my pocket and leaned over the top of the staff. Taking a breath, I pressed the precious stone into the spot that was missing a gem. As though drawn by magic, it adhered itself to the staff instantly. A high-pitched ringing sounded, and I stepped back from the statue. It lifted its staff slowly, just as the other had done, and started to speak.

"Ravens call and serpents hiss,
All hidden by starlight's kiss.
Violence and vanity,
Echoes of lost sanity.
No war cries or raised blades
Sully these shores or glades.
Shadows keep the isle free,
Thor's talisman is the key.
Accession or marriage,
Royal blood earns passage."

"Quick, write it down," I said. "Hopefully the first letters spell something out again."

With Voror's help, we wrote down exactly what the statue had said.

I frowned at the words. "Ravens..." I started to read, but Mazrith spoke over me.

"Ravensstar."

"What is that?" I looked up at him, his sharp eyes still roving over the words, but light caught my eye.

A rune was floating from one of the statues.

One of the faceless statues.

"Look!"

Mazrith whirled. "At what?"

"There's a rune. Don't you see it?"

"No. Can you read it?"

I moved cautiously as it floated past the featureless head of the statue. It was glowing purple, not the color of any rune I had ever seen before. And even though I didn't recognize the rune, somehow I did know what it said.

"Star stone?"

Mazrith let out a hiss and I turned back to him. "Do you know what we're supposed to do?"

He nodded, his expression grave. "Yes. And it is impossible."

I pulled a face. "Everything that is happening to us is impossible."

His eyes narrowed at me. "See the first half of the riddle, about ravens and snakes and no fighting?" He pointed.

"Yes."

"It is referring to an island called *Ravensstar*. A place of peaceful worship, purely for the use of the Shadow Court royal family."

"Oh. Well given that you are part of the royal family, why is that a problem?"

"You can only access it with an amulet bestowed upon my family by the gods themselves, and passed down for generations." He pointed again. "Thor's talisman."

I scanned the thongs and their amulets hanging around his neck, my optimistic resolve quavering. "I don't suppose it's one of those."

"No. It was lost with my father."

"Oh." I chewed my lip. "Surely we can get to the island another way? Can't we just take a boat?"

He gave me a long look, then sighed. "Follow me."

"I wish you had one of those magic cubes inside the palace," I panted. We had climbed more stairs than I knew the palace even had. My glimpses from the outside had shown me several tall pairs of towers joined by spindly bridges, with the central pair of spires rising higher than the others by quite a long way. I thought the cells had been high, but I was sure we were in one of the central spires now.

"Do not speak of that where others might hear you," the Prince said from in front of me.

I rolled my eyes at his back. "There's nobody here. And I don't blame them. How high are we?"

"Almost at the top."

"Which tower are your rooms in?"

"The west wing of the palace belongs to me. That encompasses two adjoining towers."

"You have a whole wing?"

"Yes."

"Why do only the Serpent Suites look different from the rest of the palace then? I assumed everything painted in that awful dried-blood color was your stepmother's."

"I have had better things to do than repaint walls," he muttered.

I shrugged. That was a fair answer.

The staircase narrowed as we moved up, and we were now in a tight spiral. It had been ages since I had seen a landing or door.

The walls were still that hateful color, though.

Eventually, the stairs ran out. One solitary stone door stood at the top, with no decoration or indication it was important.

Mazrith pushed it open, and the cool breeze of the Shadow Court swept over me. I drew in an appreciative breath. When I followed Mazrith through the door, I drew in a different kind of breath. An exclamation of awe.

We had emerged onto a bridge connecting the two spires, and the view was astonishing.

We were so high up that we were completely surrounded by nothing but an endless blanket of inky sky, *covered* with stars. They twinkled out of the gloom everywhere, sparkling and bright, a promise in the darkness.

Mazrith began to walk across the bridge, and I followed him slowly, forcing myself to look down at the mountain below, as well as around me. Past the palace walls, as far down the mountainside as I could see, a haze of forests and towns were swallowed by shifting shadow and dancing lights. My gaze snagged on the thick forest surrounding the base of the mountain, barely discernible from so high.

Were the Starved Ones down there now, staring back up at me?

Halfway across the bridge, Mazrith stopped. I leaned tentatively over the railing, looking for any kind of island in the water. Seeing none, I moved to the other side. "You can see around the entire mountain from here," I murmured, scanning the view. "But I can't see any islands. Is it hidden by your shadow magic?" Doors and caves of all sorts had been invisible in this Court until revealed by Mazrith's shadows.

"It is neither hidden, nor down there."

I turned to him, blinking slowly. "What?"

He moved to the railing, then pointed. *Up.*

I followed his extended arm.

"I'm not seeing anything."

"You need to know what you are looking for. And the easiest way is for me to show you."

I met his gaze. "You want to get in my head."

"I want to project you an image. No different than when I talk to you in your mind. Like your owl does."

I clenched my jaw, then nodded. "Okay."

His eyes flickered with what I thought was surprise but he gave me a curt nod in return.

An image floated into my head, just like when Orm had sent me images. It was nothing like the visions, no other part of me, or any of my other senses, were transported. It was just like seeing a picture in my mind.

It was of the stars, except they looked different, somehow. More solid, and together, a series of sparkling dots joining up to make... *something.*

"Note the positions of the brightest stars. They create a shape like a-"

"Crown," I breathed, seeing the constellation for myself as he said it.

"Yes."

The image faded, and I looked back out from the bridge, searching for the pattern.

The second I saw it, the stars seemed to shift. Light danced and played over the empty slice of sky, and within moments, I could make out an island. Floating in the middle of the sky, made entirely of stars, with one small but impressive building sparkling atop it.

"How is that possible? It doesn't even look solid."

"It is an illusion. It is as solid as the stone we stand on now, when you get close."

"And how do we get close?"

"The amulet activates a bridge. From right here." He tapped a hand on the railing, and I noticed a small carving of a snake, wearing a crown. I would never have spotted it, the depth of the carving too shallow to catch the moving light.

I looked back at the island, unable to keep my eyes off it as it shimmered in and out of being, a constant suggestion of not really being there.

I wanted to go there. The longing surged through me, so strong I wondered if it was part of the magic of the place.

"There must be another way to activate the bridge. Your ancestors wouldn't have just created one way, surely? What if the amulet was damaged, or lost?"

"It *is* lost," Mazrith grunted.

I looked sideways at him. "Is there any way of finding it again?" I asked tentatively, knowing how touchy he got whenever his parents were mentioned.

To my surprise, he didn't tense up or scowl. He sighed and leaned one arm against the railing, looking at the snake carving.

"To find the amulet, I would have to find my father. And I would rather he stayed wherever he was."

I stared at him. He was talking willingly. *About his parents.*

"You don't know where he is?"

Mazrith looked up at me. "What do the rumors in the other Courts say happened to him?"

"That he died in battle."

"Battle against who?"

"It varies."

"My mother died almost five years ago. My stepmother moved onto her throne mere months after that. Almost to the week, a year later, my father disappeared. The new Queen told the Court that he had decided to go on a quest to find the gods, to discover why they had abandoned us so many years ago. As proof that he had selected her to carry on ruling his Court in his absence, she wielded his staff."

"The mist-staff."

Mazrith nodded. "Yes. A fae's staff can be taken from the dead or given freely. But never stolen. As I'm sure a rune-marked knows."

"Yes," I nodded. "So, the Court believed her?"

"If they didn't, they didn't have a choice in following her. She set about spreading rumors to all the other courts that he was lost in valiant and honorable battle, telling the Shadow Court that when he returned, likely as a god himself, it would be more impressive to the rest of *Yggdrasil* if he were a glorious warrior restored from the dead."

"You think she killed him."

"Of course." He dropped my gaze to the snake again. "I hope she killed him."

My eyebrows rose. "You disliked your father."

"Dislike does not come close. He was... unkind to my mother."

"And you loved her." I knew that from my vision.

"Very much." He sighed, then looked back up at me, emotion swirling in his eyes. "The Queen may be sadistic and crazy, but that is easier to work with than my father's constant gaze. My mother had been trying to help me, but after she died, I could not continue her work while the King lived. I took his unexpected, and welcome, absence as an opportunity to do what my mother had prepared me for. To find you."

I licked my dry lips. "I'm sorry."

He quirked his eyebrows. "For what? His death? I wish I had killed him myself."

"No. For the loss of your mother. I don't have parents, but I know how I would feel if anything happened to Lhoris."

Something that may have been pain flashed over his face. "I do not deal in regret. But know that if I could have made you cooperate without threatening his life, I would have."

The words were soft and sincere, and emotion made my cheeks heat.

But he would have killed him. I knew he would.

Whatever the fates were dragging us into was bigger than Lhoris, Mazrith's mother, maybe even the two of us.

Mazrith had *had* to make me agree to help him. And he'd

had to save me from his stepmother, whatever the cost. I glanced down at the black rune on my wrist, binding me to my captor.

Would I have done the same?

"I believe you," I breathed, still staring at the rune.

He touched my cheek, and I started, looking at him. "We will see this through. And I would like it if we continued to believe each other."

I nodded, swallowing down my raging emotions. He dropped his hand slowly. Reluctantly?

"Yes," I said, nodding more vigorously. "We need to get to the island, to get the star stone. And if your father's amulet is not an option, then there has to be something else that can get us there."

Mazrith stared out at the island for a long moment, then looked back at me. "Perhaps you are right."

"I have to be right. Or this all ends here."

Shadows swirled through his irises. "We will find another way."

9

REYNA

We agreed that food would help us think and headed back to the Serpent Suites. When we reached the Prince's rooms, though, there was a royal guard waiting for him.

"My Prince," the fae said, bowing his head, then handing Mazrith a rolled-up piece of paper.

Mazrith nodded at him, and we went into his rooms. He went straight to the War room, where Brynja was laying out platters of pies. Frima, Svangrior, and Ellisar sat on one side of the massive table, and Lhoris and Kara were at the other. Kara looked distinctly more comfortable than Lhoris did about eating lunch with the shadow-fae Prince's loyal warriors.

"Maz," Frima said in greeting, shoveling a large piece of meat pie into her mouth.

He held up the scroll. "We have a message." Everybody paused and looked at him. I eased into the nearest empty chair and slowly pulled a slice of pie toward myself as he began to read the scroll aloud.

"Members of my Shadow Court, and visiting fae alike,

Rest assured that the might of this Court has been successful removing the unnatural creatures that have happened upon our borders these last nights."

Svangrior snorted an interruption. "She means, *we* stopped them moving in any further and she's sitting with her thumb up her backside, sending piss-poor fighters to corroborate your story instead of sending the entire royal guard."

Mazrith raised a brow, then continued. "It has unanimously been decided that such things as undead invasions should not interrupt the unprecedented *Leikmot*. As such, the next round of the games festival shall be held in the Ice Court in two days' time."

Everyone looked around at each other.

"Two days is not a lot. Do you think the root-river will be clear of Starved Ones?"

"It will be a dangerous journey."

"I imagine the ice-fae are leaving now, but the rest of us will travel in fleet — the Starved Ones will not stand a chance."

I only half listened to the chatter of the warriors.

We were going to the Ice Court.

During the many years I had planned to escape my masters and hide, I had created all sorts of ideas about what the other courts might be like, what secrets and marvels they may contain.

And now, I would actually see the Ice Court.

Apprehensive excitement made my stomach churn, and I ate some more pastry in an attempt to settle it.

"Is there any more?" asked Frima, gesturing at the scroll.

"Yes." Mazrith cleared his throat and continued reading. "To celebrate the commencement of the Ice Court's round in the *Leikmot,* they will be hosting a masked ball on arrival, to be followed by the first game at dawn. Signed, Queen Andask."

"You folk are obsessed with parties," I grumbled into my pie, but nobody heard me.

"Much caution should be taken during our visit to the Ice Court," said Svangrior, spooning carrots onto his plate.

"I agree. Do you see the venom in Lady Kaldar's eyes? Face like she's been slapped with a *hel*-cursed mackerel," said Ellisar.

He had a point. The hatred I had felt whenever I had seen through the ice-fae's eyes *was* fierce.

"I don't think it is Lady Kaldar we need to worry about," said Mazrith. "It is Orm who concerns me."

"Did you see the look the Queen and Orm shared when you brought in the Starved One?" I said.

Frima nodded. "They talk between themselves, I am sure of it. But even they could not have orchestrated an attack by the Starved Ones."

I looked down at my pie. They didn't know that the Starved Ones had attacked to get to me, and it was nothing to do with the Queen.

To my relief, the conversation moved on quickly to what kind of games the ice-fae might devise.

Mazrith sat down on the chair beside me and loaded his

plate. "Let us hope the games have an element of riding," he said quietly.

I smiled. "I should be so lucky. But I would love to visit Rasa before we leave, if there's time?"

He nodded. "We will ride tomorrow. Today, I have to organize my army and ensure everything is being done at the border that I instructed. The root-rivers must be safe to travel."

I nodded, realizing that I knew exactly how I wanted to spend the rest of the day. I stood up from my chair and moved to where Frima was flinging colorful insults at Svangrior.

She stopped when I reached her and raised her eyebrows. "Reyna."

"Frima." I flexed my fingers, then rested one hand on the compacted staff at my hip. "Are you, erm, busy this afternoon?"

She raised one brow. "We are at war."

"Oh."

"But my *heimskr* chief has decided we are all to be palace-bound. Apparently we are more useful here." She scowled at Mazrith, then looked back to me. "What did you have in mind?" She flicked a glance to my staff, and I realized she already knew what I wanted. She was going to make me ask for it though.

"Could we do some more training?"

"Only if you wear the war paint."

"Deal."

"You won't need that today." Frima pointed at the staff I had just pulled from its sheath. I frowned at her.

We were in the training room, I had donned the navy war paint, and I was ready to go.

"What? Why won't I need it?"

"You can ride, Reyna. You're a natural. And there's one skill that you can learn that would make a whole load of difference to you on horseback."

Excitement coursed through me. "Archery."

She nodded. "Yup. You learn to fire an arrow well, you could do a lot more damage than hitting your foes with heavy stick."

I touched my staff defensively and she laughed. "Hey, don't get me wrong, I'm not saying *don't* hit foes with heavy sticks. But another skill might go a long way."

"One of the games might involve archery," I mused.

"Another reason to learn. You'll need these for today's practice." She handed me a pair of black leather gloves. "They are spelled, so the sores on your hands should be protected."

"How?" I said, taking them from her.

"They are dwarven. Super strong." She paused, narrowing her eyes. "My mother gave them to me, so don't mess them up."

"They're yours? Thank you."

"Hm."

She set up a series of targets along the end of the room, and showed me how to hold the bow properly. I was surprised at how light it felt. Frima showed me how to notch the arrow, my arm aching as I pulled back the tight bowstring, and she tapped at my legs and arms, adjusting my stance.

I released the arrow on her command, and completely missed the target.

"Again," Frima said, before I could even give a huff of annoyance or disappointment.

I pulled a new arrow from the quiver on the floor beside me, nocked it, and took aim. Again, Frima moved my body around, lifting my elbow, lowering my chin, twisting my hips. My muscles trembled as I held the stance, waiting for her command.

"Go."

I loosed the arrow, and there was a satisfying thud when it hit the target.

A whoop of satisfaction escaped my lips, and Frima snorted. "You barely hit it." She was right, I was a fingers breadth from missing.

"But I did hit it," I grinned at her.

"Again. This time, try to get into that stance without my help."

I missed another few targets, but with Frima's guidance, I soon landed another arrow in the target.

The longer we practiced, the faster I got into the right position, and the closer to the center my arrows got.

"When you can consistently hit the target from one stance, we will practice moving around."

"Great," I mumbled, one eye closed as I took aim. If I was ever going to do this from horseback I wouldn't have the luxury of time or steadiness to perfectly tweak my position.

I released the arrow, and it landed just an inch from the center of the target.

"Good. Arm aching yet?"

I gave her a look as I lowered the bow. "It started aching on the first try."

"I forget how frail humans are," she said.

"I wish I could." At least Frima agreed I was actually human. Though she might not, if she knew about the visions.

"Do you want to stop?"

"No." I shook my head. "I'll just need a large mead with dinner."

She stepped toward me and clapped me on the back. "Good answer. Now, this time I'm going to move the target."

We practiced until I could barely hold my arm up long enough to pull the string back. I was able to hit most of the moving targets, and I had learned to put my legs into slightly different stances but keep my upper body where it needed to be for my aim to be true. When we got back to the Serpent Suites it was late, and Frima wasted no time in pouring me the promised glass of mead.

"Are you having one?" I asked her, surprised to feel disappointment that she hadn't poured herself a drink.

"No. I have to go catch up with Svangrior and Maz. You did well today."

"Thank you. For helping me."

She smiled. "Prove it in the *Leikmot*."

I nodded. "I'll do what I can."

"I know you will. Then do some more."

. . .

I had a long bath after I ate, letting the hot water seep into my aching muscles. The wounds on my hands had healed quickly, but even through Frima's gloves, they had become sore using the bow.

There was a knock on my door just as I was climbing under the covers, and I froze. What if it was Mazrith?

An undeniable part of me *wanted* it to be Mazrith.

I coughed out a "Come in!"

Brynja pushed the door open. My body deflated a little, and I forced a smile. "Hi."

"My Lady. I was asked to give you this." She came in and handed me a book. A piece of paper was sticking out of the top of it.

"By who?"

"The Prince."

She bade me goodnight and left, and I opened the book to the piece of paper. "I believe we may find something that will help us in the library tomorrow morning. Be ready at dawn. Mazrith."

I moved the paper to the side and saw that the marked page was about smelting magical talismans. Tipping the book, I checked the cover. "Enchanted and Magical Metals of *Yggdrasil*; a field guide."

Did Mazrith think we could make a new talisman?

I guessed I'd find out at dawn.

10

REYNA

When I stepped out of my room at dawn the next day, I was surprised to see Tait in the big armchair in front of the low fire. "Hi, Tait."

The shadow-spinner looked up from a book and smiled. "Good day, Reyna. You were expecting the Prince, no doubt."

I held my book up. "You got one too, huh?"

"Indeed. The Prince sent me to fetch you. He is already in the library."

I followed him out of the Serpent Suites, turning in the opposite direction than usual along the corridor.

"I guess Mazrith told you everything we have learned?" He wouldn't have invited him to the library if not, I assumed.

Tait nodded. "Yes, yes. Very interesting, all this. I simply can't fathom how long ago this trail was laid, or by whom." He slowed his pace to peer at me over his glasses. "You really don't know who your parents are?"

She's not human.

My defenses leaped up as his words swam back to me.

"No. But I'm confident they were human."

"Why?"

I opened my mouth, but found I had nothing to offer. The truth was, I had absolutely no proof at all that my parents were human.

Doubt gnawed at me. The gut-deep knowledge that I wasn't fae was all I was truly going on.

"Well, we shall find out soon enough, if we can get you two onto *Ravensstar*," he said cheerily.

"You shouldn't speak about it in the halls," I said, before even realizing I'd repeated the admonishment I had so often received.

Tait gave me a sideways grin. "You're absolutely right, of course. Especially with other fae in the palace. Honestly, I never thought I'd see the day. Cleaned me out, they have."

"Cleaned you out?"

"I've spent all my savings, then traded more, for what they've brought with them."

"What who have brought with them?"

"The ice-fae and the earth-fae! Oh, to have access to them and their belongings, it is a wonder! Normally, I have to find the fae where they are hiding in this court, and they brought little with them from their own courts, as that would give them away. But these visitors, they have all sorts of things we don't have in the Shadow Court with them!"

His enthusiasm was infectious, and I couldn't help

imagining him trading everything he owned for a stick an earth-fae told him was special somehow. "I hope you're only getting the good stuff," I told him.

"I'm no fool," he said seriously.

"Why are you so interested in things from the other Courts?"

"Are you not?"

I tilted my head in concession. "I guess. A little." *Yes.* I had been curious about the other Courts my whole life.

"Mazrith is not like his father. He allows me to explore how the magic of the others works, without fear or unmitigated resentment."

"What do you think happened to his father?" I asked, seizing on the opportunity to talk about it. We were making our way down a small, straight staircase, the walls covered in gory tapestries.

"I think the Queen killed him."

"Does the rest of the court think that too?"

"Oh, I have no idea. I tend to stay away from the palace. The Queen's demands on *shadow-spinners* are often detrimental to their health. And, in fact, their life." He gave me a grin and a shrug, then clapped his hands as we reached a landing. "Here we are."

Large wooden doors covered in carvings of books swung open when he pushed them, and we entered the library.

"Woah."

Massive oak pillars supported a vaulted wooden ceiling, carved with images of *Yggdrasil.* Bronze sconces held torches, filling the hall with the warm glow of flickering flames.

Below a gallery level sturdy bookcases towered two stories high, crammed with leather-bound tomes and ancient scrolls, every end protected by a carved snake, slithering up or down the pillar. Narrow aisles stretched between them like a maze, endings unseen in the gloom.

Huge wood-framed windows lined one wall, their glass panes framed by dense knots of iron, and tapestries between the windows showed scenes of folk performing great acts of valor.

An enormous unlit brazier was in the center of the floor, filled with the same oil I had seen in the brazier in the cave forest. Benches and tables were dotted around the cavernous space, but all of them were empty.

"Where's Mazrith?"

"Who knows. I'll be along the history section first, looking for anything about the island itself." He ambled off, and I stared around the cavernous space.

Within moments of moving, I was lost. I had no idea how to get back to the doors, and I had no idea where the history section was.

"Mazrith?" I called softly. Nobody answered. I followed the twists and turns of the shelves aimlessly, scanning titles as I went. Nothing was standing out as useful.

A strange feeling washed over me when I rounded one corner, and I turned down the row of shelves. It was a warm feeling. A curious feeling.

I kept moving, drawn to something nearby. Something that was important, that had the power to change me...

There it was. A book, standing on a shelf between two others. Nothing remarkable about it at all. But I was sure it was otherwise. I could *feel* it. I reached out for it, cocking my head, trying to control my excitement. This book would change my life. I knew it.

"Stop."

Mazrith's voice reached me at the same time his shadows flurried before me, whipping the book away from my outstretched fingers.

"Hey! I wanted to read that!" I protested. But as the book got further away, the excited desperation I'd felt faded.

I blinked at Mazrith.

"It's cursed."

"The book?"

"Yes."

"What would have happened if I'd opened it?"

"Nothing pleasant."

"Would it have killed me?"

Mazrith gave an uncharacteristic chuckle. "No. But you'd have spent the Ice ball in the bathing chamber. On the toilet."

I pulled a face. "Then thanks."

"You're welcome. You need to look for books about forging magical amulets, or about the architecture of the Shadow Court. If there is no other way to the island, we might be forced to try to recreate the talisman."

"Right. Where do we look first?"

"I've already checked the obvious places."

I looked around the massive space. "Nothing here is obvious to me. I suppose it would be to Kara. She would lose her mind in here."

"Well, if you find something that helps us, you can bring her here."

"Really?"

He looked surprised at my excitement. "Will that make you behave yourself?" I rolled my eyes, and his lips almost quirked into a smile. "You're right, nothing would make you behave. But yes. Fine. If you find what we need, bring her here."

"You'd let a *gold-giver* read everything in your Shadow Court library?"

"I'm bound to marry one," he muttered, turning away. "What does one in my library matter?"

We looked through books for what felt like hours. I stuck fairly close to Mazrith after the book-that-gave-you-the-shits incident and found myself watching him as much as the volumes.

When he found something that interested him, he changed, his gruff demeanor settling into something calm and dignified. His bright eyes scanned the pages quickly, his strong jaw working as he read.

Every time he disappeared down a new set of shelves, I darted down the opposite, watching him through the gaps.

"I know what you're doing," he said, when I thought he was engrossed in the pages of his book.

I blushed. "I'm hunting for helpful books."

"You're hunting me."

The blush deepened. "Don't be a *heimskr*," I muttered, grabbing at the closest book and pretending to read it.

"That is a book about soil potency."

"How can you tell that from the other side of the shelves?"

He appeared at the end of the row a beat later. "Magic. Or maybe just good eyesight."

"Hmm. What's your book about?" I gestured to his tome, trying to change the subject. "Anything useful?"

"Perhaps, but not in getting to the island." He held it up so I could see the cover. *Vald-staffs and their origins.*

Interest surged in me, and this time it wasn't fueled by magic. I reached for the book as I dropped the one about soil and stepped forward. "Does it have anything about Mist-staffs?"

"Yes. More than my mother told me." He paused, then handed the book to me. "Read it later. Now, we must keep looking for something that will help with the talisman or *Ravensstar*. We are short on time. We leave for the Ice Court tomorrow."

His curse and the attack by the Starved Ones were both pressing on us too.

"Sure." I took the book and tucked it under one arm.

"Did you still want to visit the stables?"

"Yes," I said, nodding vigorously. "Very much."

"Good." He paused, eyes seeming to search mine. "The Ice Court ball could be an opportunity for us."

"What do you mean?"

"There is some sort of pact between Orm and the Queen, I am sure of it. We should use the event to try to get information from anyone we can. And I believe the earth-fae Lord dislikes you much less than the others."

"Dakkar is not cruel, but I don't know that he actually likes me," I said.

"Try to get what you can from him about how he came to be here, and what the Queen offered him. Steer clear of my stepmother wherever possible. I will work on her and Orm."

"Fine by me. I'd be happy never to see the Queen again," I muttered.

"Frima has a new gown being prepared for you, suitable for the Ice Court."

I rolled my eyes. "More gowns."

"You dislike gowns?"

I cocked my head at him. "You regularly seem to forget who I am."

"You don't know who you are." The words hit me in the gut, and I stared at him as I tried to work out what to say. When I didn't speak, he added, "literally, and figuratively."

"I am Reyna Thorvald, human gold-giver," I said, slightly too loudly. "Not comfortable with gowns, balls, or *fae*." I said the last few words slowly and even more loudly, glaring at him.

"Is that who you want to be?"

I frowned. "What do you mean?"

He took a step forward, closer to me, so that I had to look up at him. "If you could be anything, what would you be? A rider? A warrior?"

I opened and closed my mouth awkwardly. What would I be if I could be anything?

Free.

Other than that, I had no idea. But I knew what I didn't want to be.

"I haven't thought about it before, but I know I don't want to be fae," I said firmly.

His eyes narrowed briefly, and he moved his braids behind his ear, deliberately showing its subtle point. "Reyna, you are a magic-user. Whether you like it or not."

"Magic-user?" My mind kicked into gear at the expression. "Wait. Can I be a magic-user and *not* be fae?" Hope surged in me, and I realized that my resistance really wasn't connected to not being human. I was scared of being fae.

"There haven't been non-fae magic users in centuries. But I believe they existed once. Does it matter?"

"What? Of course it matters."

"Why?" He stepped even closer. "Why do you need a title on the kind of person you are? Fae, human, magic-user —none of it matters. You are Reyna Thorvald, gold-giver, vision-seer, future Princess of the Shadow Court."

My legs tingled weakly at his words, his presence dominating me. "Princess," I whispered, the word tumbling through my head.

"Do you want to be a Princess?"

"It doesn't matter what I want, I have no choice in—"

"Forget your circumstances, Reyna. Forget your prejudices, your rules, your fears. Tell me what you would be if you could be anything."

"Free." My cheeks flamed with emotion, replacing tears that wanted to fill my eyes.

"Free from what? A life as a thrall?"

"From everything. Everyone."

"Your friends? Those who would…" He paused, dark eyes swirling. "Love you? Or free from visions of monsters, and masters who would abuse you?"

I swallowed, unable to answer him. Of course I wanted to be free of fae masters. But free of the visions… I had never realized how trapped they made me feel. I couldn't escape them; they were inside me.

"I don't want to be free of my friends," I said, eventually, my voice quiet.

"Good. Freedom doesn't have to be lonely."

"Are you… are you trying to say I can be bound to you, and still be free?" I shook my head. "Because that's not possible. I could never be free living in a fae palace, whether it's made of gold or shadows. I'm rune-marked, a weakling compared to everyone around me, and completely dependent on your protection. That's not freedom."

"You lie, even to yourself," he said softly. Anger flashed through me, but he continued before I could speak. "You are not weak, and you have proven to everybody in this palace that you are not completely dependent on my protection. You won the last game, and I was nowhere near you." I closed my mouth, my protestations dying on my lips. "When the Queen is dead, and Odin help me, curse or none, I will not rest until she is, then you will not need my protection."

I shook my head, but some of my conviction was gone. "I don't belong here."

Emotion lit up his eyes. Exasperation maybe? "You don't belong anywhere yet, Reyna. That is what I am trying to make you see. You are different. And when I have that mist-staff, I will remove those who would harm what they do not understand."

"You can't remove everybody," I said quietly.

"I do not need to. You will earn their respect. Just like you have earned this."

He stepped forward, closing the gap between us. The air tingled with charged energy as he reached out a hand. With a gentleness that his huge hands shouldn't have possessed, he separated a strand of my loose hair.

My breath caught, and I held it as tiny shadowy tendrils danced toward my face. They skittered through my hair, then whooshed back to his staff, and I tentatively raised my own hand as he removed his.

My finger closed over a tight, intricate braid. I stared up at the Prince's swirling eyes, then he whirled around. "Here."

He marched down the aisle, and I hurried after him. He stopped before one of the huge windows, the darkness outside enough that it was easy to see my reflection in the panes of glass.

There it was. A braid. There was nothing laced into it, like his or Frima's, as that was an honor reserved for the fae. But there was something glinting at the bottom of it, catching the firelight.

I touched the braid again, moving my fingers down its length until I reached the bead. I lifted it in front of my face, my hair easily long enough.

It was a tiny owl in silver, its huge eyes dominating the design.

I caught Mazrith's gaze in the windowpane. "Thank you."

"Thank yourself. You earned it."

I turned to him, emotion overwhelming me, but movement caught both our attention.

"Tait!" The shadow-spinner stumbled out of the aisle, blood running down the side of his face.

11

REYNA

Mazrith moved to his side, easing him down onto the nearest bench. "What happened?"

His unfocused eyes tried to lock onto Mazrith as I crouched in front of him. He had a gash above his temple, as though he had been hit.

"Someone stole my book," he stammered.

"And hit you?"

"Yes. Yes, they did that too."

Shadows rushed from Mazrith's staff, disappearing into the gloom of the expansive library. "Did you see who it was?"

"No. One minute I was lost in my reading, the next I was seeing stars and my book was pried from my fingers."

His words were getting steadier, but his face was paling as more blood trickled down his cheek.

Mazrith shrugged off his cloak, a heavy black woolen affair, and tore a strip off the bottom as though it were

82

parchment. He rolled it up before pressing it to Tait's wound, just as white wings fluttered above us.

"Voror!" He landed on the table and blinked at me.

Tait stared. "Is there an owl in here?" he whispered, touching his hand to his head.

"Yes," I told him. "Voror, did you see who hit Tait?"

"I was worried about the imminent exchange of bodily fluids between you two, so I had settled high in the rafters," he said. My cheeks burned.

"He saw nothing," I said, turning back to Mazrith.

"What book did they take?" he asked Tait.

"It was about the history of the Shadow Court palace and the mountain. But my Prince, it wasn't the book that they were after." A triumphant gleam came into his dazed eyes. "There was a piece of parchment inside the book."

Mazrith stilled. "Do you still have it?"

"Yes, although I wouldn't need it."

My confusion grew, but before I could ask, shadows flowed back to Mazrith's staff. His face tightened with frustration. "Whoever it was left too fast for my shadows to catch them."

"Who has access to this library?" I asked.

"Half the Court," he answered darkly. "Tait, do you need immediate attention? Or can you tell us more?"

He waved a slightly wobbly hand dismissively. "The piece of parchment was one of a few, hidden in books inside the library. They contain the rune-words needed to get into your father's armory. But I know them all."

"His armory?" I asked.

Tait nodded, then stopped with a wince. Mazrith pulled

the fabric back, and I saw with relief that the bleeding had stopped.

"I knew it was somewhere in this library," Mazrith said quietly. "But I was never invited to visit it and have had no desire to do so since his death."

"Is someone else looking for it?"

"Or trying to keep us from entering it." Mazrith looked between me and Tait. "If there is any chance my father did not have the talisman on his person when he left, then we might find it in his private armory."

I raised my eyebrows. "Did he usually wear it?"

"No. It was heavy and valuable. Inappropriate for battle." Mazrith looked thoughtful. "I do not know how she caused his death, but if my stepmother sent him into some sort of fight there is a chance the talisman is still in the palace."

I blew out a breath. "Let's find his armory then."

We followed Tait slowly up one of the spiraling staircases to the gallery floor, then to one of many carved snake pillars at the end of an aisle of bookcases. Voror glided behind us, no longer staying hidden.

Tait reached out, touching the snake's lifeless wooden eye. "A shadow here, my Prince."

Shadows flowed from Mazrith's staff and zoomed into the eye of the serpent. It glowed green, and a creaking sounded from between the shelves of books. We made our way down the aisle to a tapestry at the end showing a

COURT OF MONSTERS AND MALICE

shadow-fae staff with a skull on the top, very similar to Mazrith's. He cocked his head when he saw it, his shoulders tightening. "My mother's staff," he said quietly.

Tait nodded. "*Veita,*" He said. I didn't know the word, but the tapestry shimmered and then disappeared, replaced with a wooden door with the exact same image carved into it.

Mazrith pushed the door open.

It looked more like a study to me than an armory.

A modest sized space, the walls were painted deep gray, and lit by sconces like the rest of the library. A large leather-covered desk was covered in papers and trinkets, an ivory horn on a stand taking up a good third of it. A fireplace with no wood in it. But a bear's head mounted on a board above it was hard to ignore, and I blinked at it.

"That bear is red."

"Father claimed he killed fire-bears in the Fire Court. Some believed he painted a normal bear red."

I dragged my eyes from it and raked them over the rest of the room. Most of the walls were lined with cabinets, shelves filled with both functional things like tumblers and bottles, and items that were meant to be displayed. Most of them were weapons, I guess giving it the 'armory' name.

"Do you see the talisman anywhere?"

"No. But it was not large. It is in the shape of *Mjolnir.*"

I looked around for anything shaped like Thor's legendary hammer, but could see nothing. Mazrith began shuffling through the papers on the desk, and Tait eased himself into the only chair, looking a little awkward.

"I wouldn't deign to sit in the king's seat, except my head is a little fuzzy—"

Mazrith waved at him, not looking up from his papers. "Piss on his grave, if you knew where his body lay," he muttered. "I care not."

Voror had landed on top of a high shelf, pecking at a horned helmet that gleamed with emeralds. "This does not belong here. It is from the Earth Court," he tutted.

A small ornament on a shelf had caught my attention, and I moved to it. A man on one knee holding an axe as large as himself.

It was the berserker. I reached to pick it up, and opened my mouth to ask Mazrith about it, but as my fingers closed around the cool stone, my vision clouded, then darkened completely.

I was inside the trunk of *Yggdrasil*, but everything was so gloomy I could barely see. There were steps rising out of the water, between two set of Court doors, but I couldn't make out which ones.

The vision lifted and I realized I had stumbled into Mazrith. "Are you getting a vision?" I nodded, and he gripped my arm.

The darkness fell again.

I was high up this time. Still inside the tree, looking down over the heads of the enormous central statues from a small, earthy platform. Vertigo took me, and very real nausea clenched my throat. The darkness lifted, the dead king's armory coming back into focus.

"The tree," I murmured. "*Yggdrasil*." My vision changed again, the third wave taking me.

A huge, bearded man with dozens of braids was on his knees in front of me, fierce concentration lining his beautiful fae face. The gloom was hard to see through, but he was closing something. A chest?

The vision lifted, and for the first time in my life, I prayed for a fourth wave. But none came.

"Reyna?" Mazrith was gripping my arm tightly.

I shook my head. "You can let go," I said.

He did, reluctantly, and I put the little statue back on the shelf, my mind racing.

"Are you in pain? Fear?" He sounded as confused as he did concerned.

"No. No, I'm fine. It wasn't a vision of the Starved Ones."

I had seen the fae with the braids before, in another vision. I had seen him giving the mist-staff to the Queen, and I had been sure he was Mazrith's father. But now I questioned that. If the Queen had killed him to take his staff, then the vision I had seen of him handing it over freely made no sense.

Maybe what I was seeing weren't memories, or things that had actually happened? But I had seen Mazrith as a child, and the conversation he'd had with his mother, and they had definitely been real.

"What did you see?"

I turned slowly back to Mazrith, aware of Tait staring intently at us both from his chair, and Voror's unblinking gaze.

Carefully, I told them what I had seen. "Do you think it was your father I saw?"

"From your description, yes. It could be." His expression was tight.

I hesitated before speaking again. "If that's the case, and these visions are of real things that have happened, then he gave the mist-staff willingly to your stepmother."

Mazrith's hard gaze bore into me. "I have thought about that since you told me of the previous vision."

It hadn't even occurred to me before. But for Mazrith... It meant the man he hated so much and believed dead may still be alive somewhere.

"Perhaps the Queen tricked him into giving it to her," I offered. "Then killed him."

"It must have been quite some trick, to give up one of the world's rarest and most powerful weapons," he said darkly.

"Women are good at getting what they want from men," I said. His gaze sharpened. "Not me," I added, holding up my hands. "Seduction is not one of my strengths." I swallowed, my cheeks flushing. "Anyway, what do you think I saw him doing in the tree? It looked like he was getting something from a chest."

Mazrith's eyes shone. "You said you saw a staircase in the wood?"

"Yes. Intricately carved, and it wound up the inside of the tree."

Tait spoke. "I have heard rumors that the tree can present its interior as it wishes. Perhaps the staircase can be revealed somehow. The King may have discovered that there was something hidden inside the tree and gone to retrieve it."

"Or hidden something of his own in there," said Voror.

I snapped my eyes to the owl. "You think he put the talisman in there?"

Mazrith gave a thoughtful grunt. "He may have wanted to hide his valuables outside of the Shadow Court. Many of his possessions went missing with him. But it is a flimsy theory."

Voror's feathers bristled. "I am a wise and superiorly intellectual owl. My ideas are not *flimsy*. You saw that vision for a reason."

I didn't relay his words to the Prince. "Why do you think touching the statue gave me the vision?" I asked instead.

"I have no idea."

We all fell silent.

"I do not mean to be inconvenient, but I am developing a headache I am struggling to ignore," said Tait eventually. "And I feel a little sick."

We both moved to him, helping him stand. "I'm sorry, friend," Mazrith said gently. "We will take you to the Serpent Suites, and I will return here to search for anything of help." He looked at me. "We must continue to try to find another way onto *Ravensstar* or create a new amulet. Bring all the books we found."

12

REYNA

"Are you sure we should leave him?" I asked as we headed down the corridor, toward the stables.

We had taken Tait to the Serpent Suites and left him in the care of Ellisar and Kara. Both had seemed willing and capable, but I felt bad. He had been hurt helping us.

"What would you do that they cannot?" Mazrith asked, giving me a sideways look.

I shrugged. "Nothing, I suppose."

"Then we practice your riding."

The stablemaster looked surprised to see us when we entered the stables, leaping up from a fold-out table with a steaming mug on it and bowing low to Mazrith.

"My Prince, I did not know you would need Jarl today. He is recovering well from the long ride to the borders, but I am not sure he will desire a vigorous run today."

"Jarl will take his rest. I will ride Idunn today."

The stablemaster flicked his gaze to me. "And the Lady?"

"She wishes to see Rasa."

The stable master swallowed, his brown beard bobbing obviously. "Rasa may not wish to be ridden."

"I know. We will see how a conversation with her goes first."

"As you wish."

He walked us toward a stall nervously, though Mazrith clearly already knew where he was going. When we reached the swing doors to the pen, his hand paused by the bolt that opened them.

"Go and ready Idunn. I will manage this," Mazrith said.

"My Prince," he said gratefully and hurried off.

Mazrith turned to me. "You sure you want to do this?"

I heard hooves still behind the doors, then a snickering. "Yes."

He pulled the bolt and then eased the stall doors open.

Rasa flicked her tail, slowly lifting her head to blink one large eye at me.

I lifted my hand awkwardly, then remembered I was supposed to be confident. I squared my shoulders, and she pawed at the ground with her front hoof.

"Hi," I said.

She turned in the stall, to face me, then gave a long, loud neigh. It didn't sound friendly.

"Sorry I left in a hurry after the race," I told her.

She took a few steps forward. I held my ground.

"My friends were in trouble. I feel like you would protect your friends, so you understand that, right?"

Voror's voice entered my mind. "She's a horse. She

doesn't understand anything you're saying. She does not have the superior intellect an owl has."

I ignored him, focusing instead on Rasa's large, approaching form. "Do you fancy another run?"

The horse stopped, flicking her tail again, then shaking her head hard from side to side.

Was that a yes or a no?

With sudden speed she moved, dashing out of the stable pen. I leaped to the side in time, feeling Mazrith's hand on my shoulder as I did.

Once in the open area in the middle of the large stables, she began to trot in a circle, bucking her back legs every few paces.

Mazrith sighed. "This is what she does when I try to talk to her. It usually takes three of us to get her back in."

"Can you not use your shadows?" I asked quietly, trying not to feel so disappointed in the horse's reaction to me.

"They make her even worse."

"That's weird, given that your mom used to ride her. You'd think she would be used to shadows."

He gave me a hard look, and I regretted mentioning his mom. But his look softened. "I think that's why she doesn't like them," he said.

"They trigger her grief? Can horses even feel grief?"

"I believe so," he said, watching Rasa buck and canter in a wide circle.

"They certainly do," said Voror in my head.

"Voror, do you know what might calm her down?" I asked aloud. Mazrith gave me glance but said nothing.

"She is a creature of instinct and reckless abandon," he

said distastefully. "I share little knowledge with a beast like her."

"Well, what do her instincts want?"

"The same as the last time we were in her presence."

"Freedom," I breathed.

I took a few steps toward the horse, Mazrith by my side.

"Rasa!" I called. The horse ignored me. "Want to burn off some of that fire with me again?"

She rocked to a halt, swinging her head a few times before settling it to look at me.

"We can go just as fast, but there will be less folk trying to kill us. That sound good?"

She turned on the spot, snorting.

"But you have to come back when it's time. That's part of the deal."

She bucked again, resuming her circles.

"And if it goes well we can keep going out!" I tried to keep the desperate note from my voice. "Outside these stables, in the trees and the fresh air. As much as you like. As long as you come back each time."

She had slowed as I had spoken, and when I finished, she moved slowly toward us.

As she got within a few feet, I felt the cold trickle of Mazrith's shadows and realized he was ready to protect us if she kicked or bolted.

Sucking up confidence from that, I stepped forward, my hand outstretched. She ignored my hand, turning instead so that her flank was to me.

"What does that mean?" I whispered to Mazrith.

"That we should saddle her quickly, before she changes her mind."

I wouldn't say Mazrith and the stablehand had an easy job of getting Rasa ready, but there were no broken limbs. She was twitchy when I mounted her, rocking alarmingly at first. But every time I told her she could go as fast as she wanted once we were outside the stable, she settled.

Part of me was sure I would regret telling her that. If I fell off in the haunted forest, I would be in serious trouble. If I fell off anywhere else, I had a high chance of serious injury. I looped my hands through the reins twice, just in case, and settled my feet firmly in the stirrups.

"Don't throw me," I told her, as Mazrith and Idunn moved ahead, toward the slowly opening doors. "If you throw me, we don't get to go out again."

She tipped her head back, snorting.

"Are you ready—" Mazrith started to say from in front of me. But I never heard him finish. Before the doors were fully open, Rasa was off.

My breath left me in a rush, and I didn't have any time at all to try to settle into her rhythm. I just clung on for dear life.

"Stand in your stirrups, bend your knees and grip her shoulders, and keep those reins in your hands," Mazrith's voice said inside my head.

I sucked in cold air, the gnarled trees whipping past me, and tried to do as he told me.

I managed to lift my backside from the saddle, leaning low over her neck and squeezing with my knees. I was immediately more comfortable and risked a glance over my shoulder.

Mazrith and Idunn were behind us, Idunn's hooves pounding the forest path, but unable to keep up with Rasa.

"Blessed Freya, you're fast," I told her. If it were possible, I was sure she sped up. My hair flew out behind me, her hooves eating the ground beneath us. The flow of her movements became rhythmic enough that I could fall into them, and a broad smile took my lips.

Tumbling thoughts about who had hurt Tait, how I would survive the *Leikmot*, the evil Queen, the hideous Starved Ones, my confused emotions about the prince, my own missing identity, even — none of them could get through the barrier of rushing wind Rasa was creating. She was faster than my thoughts; they couldn't keep up. And I would outrun them for as long as I was able.

When we burst out of the forest just moments later, Rasa didn't slow. And I didn't tell her to. She pounded through the streets, people darting out of the way. They needn't have— her nimble body wove between carts or folk walking without barely having to slow.

Some people shook their fists at me as I passed but she was too quick for me to see them properly. And I didn't care.

She galloped on once we left the village, toward the forest I had practiced jumping in with Idunn. I didn't know what was beyond the forest. "Don't go all the way through the forest, Rasa," I called to her. "Keep the pace, but stay in the trees."

I had no idea if she understood me, but when we entered the dense foliage, she did slow to a canter before leaving the well-worn path straight through.

She leaped over fallen logs and sometimes even whole bushes, and turned tight corners to dart between trees, like she was able to see them coming before I did. Her instinctive agility was amazing, and I let her lead us, doing nothing with the reigns or my legs to guide her.

After a while she slowed to a trot, stopping to snap her jaws at low-flying insects and butterflies hovering over a bush with bright red berries and orange flowers. I ran my hand along her neck without thinking, and she froze a moment, then shook her head and continued trying to catch butterflies.

"You're not born to stay cooped up in that stable," I muttered.

"With you able to ride her like that, she won't have to be anymore." The Prince's voice was a tiny bit breathless, but made me jump all the same.

"You kept up, then?" I turned in my saddle to see him ten feet away. Idunn was breathing hard.

"Barely."

I grinned. "I wager you a whole bottle of nettle wine that I make it back before you then. Come on, Rasa!"

13

REYNA

I should have bet him something better, like a whole bottle of mead, because I made it back to the stables a full five minutes before he did.

"If I were riding Jarl, you would have had better competition," he growled when he pulled Idunn to a stop next to me.

"Uh-huh." I couldn't stop smirking as he conjured a shadowy step to help me dismount Rasa. As soon I was off her back, Mazrith leaped down to remove her saddle.

"Thanks for coming back," I told the horse.

She eyed me as Mazrith worked quickly. But the tension from her body was gone, and her snorts had lost their vigor.

"We've been challenged to another race by the loser here," I said.

She flicked her tail.

"So I'll be back in a few days."

She neighed.

"I think that means challenge accepted," I told Mazrith, as we led her to her stall.

"I can see how you earned that braid," he said, bolting her pen, then looking at me. "You two belong together."

My cheeks flushed, pleasure mixing with the adrenaline. "I love riding her."

"A rider, then?"

"What?"

"What you would be, if you could be anything."

"She makes me feel free." It was a simple statement, but somehow felt like I was sharing a secret.

His eyes bore into mine, and the memory of the fierce kiss we had shared in this very space filled my head.

I almost took a step backward, to stop myself moving forward.

Kissing him would be a terrible idea. Wouldn't it?

My feet moved. Toward him.

He took a step back and I halted.

His expression changed, the emotion draining away. "I look forward to our next race," he said, sweeping his cloak out behind him and walking toward Idunn.

I waited a moment before following him, letting my racing pulse settle. I was exhilarated from the ride and mixing that up with passion.

He was right to stop anything from happening. We had precious little time to find the mist-staff, and we couldn't afford any more fights or emotional entanglements.

He hasn't really forgiven you for lying to him, said a little voice in the back of my head.

I took a breath and tried to wrangle my thoughts under control. So much for outrunning them.

I turned and made my way to the Prince, who was running a brush over Idunn's coat.

"Should I be doing that for Rasa?"

"You'll have to build up to that, I think."

"Okay. When can we come back?"

"I wish I knew," he answered darkly.

"How long do you think we will be in the Ice Court for?"

He shrugged. "The games here were over four days. I hope for the same. I do not wish to be away too long."

"Because of the Starved Ones attacking?"

He glanced around the stables, but they appeared empty. "They will not attack while you are not here."

I swallowed, my skin prickling. "Right."

"No, I want to get to *Ravensstar* island and fix the statue. And I can't do that from outside the Shadow Court."

We ate as a group again, in the war room. Tait joined us too, a bandage around his head but in seemingly high spirits.

Mazrith and the warriors talked about the preparations for leaving the Court the next morning, and I listened while I ate a spiced meat stew that was nicer than anything I had ever eaten in the Gold Court.

"Svangrior has selected a slew of weapons from the armory this afternoon, and I spent a few hours in the thrall quarters, going over the palace canvases, in case we need them. Nothing has been tampered with, and I oversaw everything being stowed on the *Knarr* personally," Frima said.

"What is the *Knarr*?" I asked.

"The longboat we will be traveling in. It is a cargo vessel built for longer voyages, and has enough cabins for our party," Mazrith answered.

I looked at him. "We are all going, I assume?"

He paused, then shook his head. "With the Queen leaving the Shadow Court, I think it is safest to keep your friends here."

I swallowed back my immediate argument. Was he right? Much as I didn't want to be apart from them, it was likely to be more dangerous for my friends where the games were, given the stunt the Queen had just pulled. Everyone involved had seen that they were important to me now, so they could be targets.

I looked at Kara and Lhoris. "Are you both okay with that?"

Kara nodded, but Lhoris spoke. "Will someone be staying with us here or will we be locked in the thrall quarters again?"

"Ellisar will stay here with you," Mazrith told him.

"I will?" The big man looked a little disappointed.

"Yes. I anticipate little trouble, and you recently received a head injury."

"Wait, you're leaving him here to keep them safe, and you think he is unfit?" I protested.

"He will not be alone. There are a number of palace guards loyal to me. Not to be trusted as my warriors are," he added pointedly, "but reliable enough to aid Ellisar if he needs it."

Ellisar bashed his chest, scowling. "I am fit for the task."

Mazrith nodded. "I know. But a cold climate is not a place for a human to heal." He looked to the shadow-spinner. "Tait, I'm sorry, but despite your injury, I *will* need you to join us."

He nodded enthusiastically. "I would have stowed away if you had refused me passage."

"You are not there to load up my ship with trinkets and toys," Mazrith said sternly. "You are there to repair my staff if the worst should happen."

"Of course, my Prince," he said, then tore into his bread with a childlike expression of excitement on his elderly face.

"Do you have any idea who might have followed you to the library this morning?" Frima asked Mazrith, looking at Tait's bandage.

"None. Although I am willing to bet it is the same person who has been trying to harm Reyna."

The warriors didn't know about what had happened in the shrine, but they did know about the snake left in my room.

"It must be someone close to the party, to have access to so much information, and these rooms," growled Svangrior.

I stared at him until his eyes met mine. I thought about holding his gaze, making the challenge, but I dropped it to my food instead. I had no proof it was him. Just a reluctance to believe it was Frima or Ellisar.

"We must be on our guard, always," Mazrith said. "And nobody travels anywhere alone." He looked pointedly at me.

ELIZA RAINE

I shrugged and waved my hand at him, the serpent ring glinting. "I'm not going anywhere without you knowing about it."

"Knowing where you are does not help me keep you alive," he growled.

"I didn't think I could leave these rooms without magic," I said.

He narrowed his eyes at me. "You can't, but that hasn't stopped you before."

I paused. Did he know about the escape attempt, and my accidental meeting with Arthur? Unless the warriors had told him, I couldn't see how.

Without leaving my eyes, he said, "We will not be taking any horses, or Arthur, with us, as there's no room on the ship and I do not perceive us needing them in a tundra."

Oh fates. He knew.

"Shame. Arthur is handy to have around," I said, nonchalantly.

"Is Arthur the bear with the shield you told me about?" Kara asked quietly.

Seizing the opportunity to look away from the Prince, I turned to her. "Yes. He is very impressive. Have you read about any other magical animals?"

Mercifully, Mazrith let me talk to Kara for the rest of the meal, discussing travel preparations with Svangrior and Frima instead.

He left the meal first, to see to the guards, and when I retired to my own bedroom, I found myself restless. Excitement about the journey was part of it, I was sure, but another thought kept creeping in.

102

Earlier, Mazrith had mentioned magic-users. And the term had kept coming back to me. Was it possible that my parents, or one of my parents, had been something that wasn't fae or human?

Silently, I padded to Kara and Lhoris' room. I slipped in without knocking, making Kara startle.

"Reyna!" she gave a surprised whisper. Lhoris was asleep in the big armchair. I beckoned her out of the room, and she followed me back to mine.

"What's wrong?" she asked when I closed my door.

"Nothing. I just wanted to ask for your help. Again."

"Of course." She sat down next to me on the bed.

"While I'm gone, do you think you could look for information about magic-users that are not fae, especially who might get visions or use mind-magic?"

Her face lit up. "In the library? Of course I can! Wait." Her smile faded. "Is this the same library Tait was attacked in?"

"Yes. So you mustn't go alone. Only go with Ellisar. And tell him you're doing research for the Prince."

She nodded. "I can do that."

"Thank you."

"Are you worried about the ice games?"

I was about to say no, but something in her expression made me pause. I had always presented myself to her as strong because I wanted her to learn to look after herself. But since coming here, I had seen that she had courage already. And perhaps skills that would keep her alive that were nothing like my own. She was tolerant, amenable, and had a wisdom beyond her years.

"Yes. A little," I admitted. "And I'm not used to the cold."

She smiled and ran her hands over the many bed coverings. "There will be no shortage of furs, I'm sure."

"True. Lady Kaldar does not like anybody in these games. I'm a bit worried she will try to do something."

Kara shook her head. "She may be the Ice Court champion, but she is not in charge of it."

"You're right. I'll meet the King and Queen of the Ice Court," I realized.

She looked a little wistful. "I sort of wish I was going with you. But I don't like the cold either."

"I think Mazrith is right, and you will both be safer here. How is Lhoris doing?"

"He gets quieter every day, but I think he is fine. He is struggling with his own thoughts, I believe."

"He's not the only one," I muttered. "And you?"

She shrugged. "I find my thoughts challenged in a good way. And now I get to explore a library. Is it a big one?"

"Yes. And it has a fire pit."

Once Kara had left, I was not surprised when Voror swooped down to land on the bed post.

"So, superiorly intellectual one," I greeted him. "How do you think we should get onto the impossible island? Find another way, or recreate the talisman?"

"You must find the original talisman. It was made by the gods. You can not recreate it." He clicked his beak. "Your

Prince knows this, but he does not wish to search for his father."

"Do you think the King is still alive?"

"No. He would not have left his Court for so long if he was."

I nodded. "You still think that vision showed me where he hid the talisman?"

"Why would my mind have changed?" He tilted his head at me in apparent confusion. "Humans are strange."

I sighed. "I thought you said I wasn't human."

"You speak like one. That is strange enough for now. I wish to speak with you about the Ice Court."

I crossed my legs under me on the bed. "Go ahead."

"I may be strong and stealthy and wise," he said, shifting his weight between his spindly taloned legs.

My heart sank as I guessed what he was going to say next. "But..."

"But I am not able to survive cold temperatures."

I slumped my head, chin meeting my chest. "I understand," I mumbled.

He clicked his beak. "You are sorry I will not be able to accompany you?"

I lifted my head to look at him. "Yes. I like having you watching my back. You saved my life."

"The Prince and his uncouth Lady warrior will watch your back in the Ice Court."

I took a deep breath. "I know. But I like talking to you too."

A funny little ripple moved through his feathers. "You

are too stupid to be entirely stimulating conversation, but I have grown to enjoy your company."

I gave him a look. "Couldn't help calling me stupid even when being nice to me, huh?"

Ignoring me, he carried on. "I believe I can be of much more use to you in a different way while you are engaged in the *Leikmot*."

"Really?"

"Yes. I will accompany you to the tree of *Yggdrasil*, and wait for you there."

Realization washed over me. "You want to look for the King's chest inside the tree."

"Yes."

"You're not lying about the cold killing you just so that you can prove to the Prince that your ideas aren't *flimsy*, are you?"

"Absolutely not. However, when I am proved right, I expect you to take sufficient time to extract an apology from him."

"Voror, if you find Thor's talisman, I'm quite sure he'll do more than apologize to you. He may even kiss you."

I grinned as the owl spread his wings wide, twisting his head in obvious disgust. "Then I retract my offer of help."

"Fine. I'll make sure he doesn't kiss you."

He flew up into the rafters, his voice floating to me as he left. "I would advise you not to let him kiss you either. It seems to make both of you behave even more strangely than usual."

14

REYNA

It was hard to say goodbye to Kara and Lhoris the following morning. Whilst nobody said it, we were all painfully aware that there was a chance I wouldn't come back. Mazrith would do what he could to keep me alive, but he couldn't get involved in the actual games. Perhaps the Ice Court wouldn't design games so clearly unsuitable for a human.

Yeah, right.

"Earn another braid, Reyna," said Kara, hugging me.

Lhoris lifted my new braid and beamed at me. "By Thor, earn three," he said, before pulling me into him. He was not a man who hugged often, so I leaned hard into him, savoring the feeling. "Be careful. I know you trust him, but nobody here is our ally," he murmured into my hair.

"I will. I promise."

. . .

Svangrior and Frima bickered as we made our way through the palace, Tait and Brynja following behind us. I walked next to Mazrith, who was silent. He wore his skull mask, and when we left the palace through the main doors, I realized why. Hundreds of fae and humans alike had come to see the royal contingent leave the Court.

It had been a long time since fae had been invited to visit other Courts, rather than raiding them in the darkness, so I could understand the excitement.

A basic, open sided carriage drawn by four horses waited at the bottom of the steps, and the six of us climbed onto the wooden platform. Hard benches offered somewhere to sit.

"Wait, why is the Queen going to the Ice Court, when none of the royals from the other Courts came here?" I asked, the thought only just occurring to me.

Mazrith gave me a dark look as the horses began to move without instruction. "I would imagine the others did not feel comfortable enough to leave their Courts unprotected. It would not be unwise to suspect a trap — that the games were a ploy to lure them from their thrones."

"And she doesn't feel that way?"

"She instigated all of this. Though I suppose the others could take advantage."

"With you both away, who's in charge?"

"She left Rangvald here."

"Huh." He hadn't seemed all that powerful. Smart, but not strong.

As if sensing my thoughts, Mazrith spoke wryly. "Do not underestimate him. He presents what he believes people want to see. The true nature of that man is hidden under layers of obsequious horseshit."

"The fates haven't spoken a truer word," snarled Frima. "That man is a turd."

"Do you trust him to look after your Court?" I asked Mazrith.

"No. But he is smart enough to hold it until I can return."

Frima punched Mazrith on the shoulder. "It won't come to that, I'm sure. We'll be in and out of the Ice Court." The tension in her face didn't match the light tone of her voice. She didn't know that the Starved Ones would follow me to the Ice Court. The only real threat *here* would be from rival fae.

"Hold onto something, we're about to move through the forest," Svangrior barked from the row of benches in front.

Brynja gave a small squeak as the horses abruptly picked up speed, and we began to hurtle through the haunted forest.

Despite leaving and entering the palace a few times now, I had not traveled the conventional route before, down the outside of the mountain.

I found myself fascinated as we spiraled our way down through at least ten different villages. They all had a distinct identity, some smelling of smelted metal and ringing with the clangs of smiths, others lined with stretched skins on frames, humans beating them with clubs. Others seemed to be devoted to cooking, long tables in front of buildings lined with vegetables and folk chopping and filling sacks. Everyone we passed stopped to look, but barely any waved or nodded. I wondered if they had shown more love for their Prince before he had aligned himself with me. The red-headed, human outcast.

But when I glanced at his stoic, masked face, his huge and solid form pressed to my side, I also wondered if I cared. Without me, they would lose their Prince to his curse and be left to the rule of a madwoman.

Forests dotted the gaps between the villages, and some had trees and shrubs similar to the ones in the cave that glistened with ethereal light in the constant twilight.

When we reached the forest at the bottom of the mountain, the atmosphere shifted. I had been in this forest before, and it wasn't friendly. Even without undead creatures chasing me through it, I could feel the defensive energy coming from the trees that guarded the mountain.

The carriage kept moving us through the foliage, following a wide path that emerged onto a shore of black sand, and the start of the root-river. But I didn't even notice the water. My gaze was fixed on the largest longboat I had ever seen. Brynja and I both gasped when it came into view.

Frima gave me a grin. "Isn't she beautiful?"

She was. The sturdy oak hull must have measured over fifty feet from end to end, though it was shallow and low to the water. An elaborately carved serpent figurehead twisted at the front, as if ready to plunge into the waves, similar to the one on the *karve* that had brought me to the Shadow Court, but so much bigger.

"Time for the tour," Frima said, vaulting from the carriage as soon as the horses came to a stop. I followed her, and Svangrior reluctantly helped Brynja down. The girl looked a little overwhelmed, but Frima gave me no time to check on her. "Come," she said, stepping onto a small ramp that allowed easy access to the deck, which was wide enough for three wooden cabins, each with shuttered windows and a sloping roof.

The center cabin was the largest, and more snakes had been burned into the wooden doors and window shutters. Mazrith's cabin, I guessed. I peeked inside and saw a bed covered in furs and three large chests with padlocks. A basin stood in the corner, but I couldn't imagine there was running water.

The cabins on either side were only slightly smaller, still spacious enough to be comfortable. One was filled with shields and weapons hanging from the walls, secured with ropes.

"This sail was made by the ancient royal family. Mazrith's grandfather himself fashioned it." Frima slapped her hands to the massive mast in the center of the deck and looked up at the huge sail.

"And if that goes to horseshit, there's always the oars," grumbled Svangrior, barging past me to get to the cabin with the weapons. "Tait, you're with me," he called back over his shoulder, before slamming the door.

"Lucky Tait," I mumbled.

I caught a flash of white wings over the top of the cabins, confirming that Voror had made it with us.

"In case you need to know, there are extra sails, ropes, tar, wood, food, weapons — and a load of other shit — under the decking, in the belly of the ship. The trapdoor is where Maz is standing." The back of the ship had a raised platform and Mazrith's fur-clad form was still as he looked out over the water.

"Okay. Am I... Am I sharing a cabin with you?" I already knew the answer, but I thought I'd ask.

Frima snorted. "What, and Maz shares with Brynja?" At that exact moment, Brynja walked up with a small bag, and the color drained from her face.

"It's okay, Brynja, she's joking," I said quickly.

Frima gave her an only slightly apologetic smile. "You're in with me," she told the girl.

Brynja didn't look as relieved as I thought she would. I couldn't blame her. Frima had her moments of being pretty scary. I glanced at Mazrith, still staring broodily, skull mask glinting. Hm. Maybe Frima wasn't so bad.

"My ladies, where is food prepared?" Brynja's voice was barely audible, and I felt bad for her. She had been fairly confident when there were no shadow-fae around. Maybe this journey and the forced proximity would help her see they weren't a threat.

Frima moved to a long chest lining one side of the main deck, opened the lid, and hauled out a long piece of flat wood. "Want to help?" She threw an annoyed glance at me, and I moved, helping her fold out what I realized was a large table. Once we dragged it to a bench fixed to the deck, Brynja sat down, removed carrots from her bag, and a small knife. Tait emerged from the cabin he had followed Svan-grior into and sat beside her.

"We are leaving now," Mazrith called from the platform. He raised his staff and shadows whirled from it. They rushed toward the sail, filling it, stretching it taut. With a lurch, the ship began to move.

15

REYNA

The excitement of moving along the river wore off surprisingly quickly. I could see nothing in the void over the edges of the root-river, and the boat was large enough that we barely even rocked on the gentle surface. I offered to help Brynja prepare vegetables, but she refused, saying it was no job for a Lady, and ignoring my protestations that I was no such thing.

Tait had brought a stack of books out to the table and was reading one. Both Frima and Svangrior were sharpening weapons.

After a while, Mazrith came down from his platform. His grey eyes flashed as I watched him remove his mask.

"I sense no Starved Ones, nor can my shadows find any ahead," he said. I felt some of my restlessness ease. "I recall you promising to read, every spare moment you had," he said to me, looking pointedly at Tait's stack of books.

Svangrior looked up from his axe. "You can read?"

I bristled, but it was a fair assumption that I couldn't. Few but nobility could. "Kara taught me the basics."

"How did she learn?" asked Tait, interested enough to look up from his volume.

"She was a maid in a household with a son the same age. He shared his lessons with her. Until her rune-mark presented itself, and she was brought to the palace."

Tait nodded and went back to reading. Mazrith picked up the top book from the stack. "Smelting and Forging with Precious Gems."

He handed it to me, then picked up the next one. "I will be in my cabin." As he strode off, Frima set her sword down.

"Why are you all reading books about forging? Wedding jewelry?" She flashed me a smile.

I looked uncomfortably at the cabin door that had just closed, and saw it open a crack.

"Mind your own, Frima," Mazrith's voice called.

She pulled a face at the door after it closed again. "He's cheerful today."

As a group, we fell into silence, focusing on our tasks as we powered down the river. Periodically, Brynja made us nettle tea using a small brazier near the front of the ship, and a meal of hard cheese and soft bread was handed out. Mazrith didn't leave the cabin, even for the food.

Reading made me sleepy, only about two thirds of the words familiar to me and none of it very interesting. I believed Voror wholeheartedly that we couldn't forge a new talisman, though I was less optimistic about the original one being hidden inside the tree of *Yggdrasil*.

The visions I had gotten so far that hadn't featured the

Starved Ones had all been connected to the quest to find the mist-staff, so he could be right. Someone was sending them to me, and I yearned to know who. Voror's mystery-fae seemed the most likely, but I couldn't tell anyone about her.

I stared down at the boring, probably useless, book. Mazrith had the ones about using magic to cross large expanses of open air, which would likely be more helpful. I wished I was reading the book about mist-staffs, but I'd stupidly left it behind.

I dozed off, my head on my arms on the table, and jerked awake when Svangrior banged his axe on the wooden planks.

"The gates of *Yggdrasil* are close," he said loudly. "I'll get Maz."

The root-river had closed in over us, dense canopies of sparkling leaves overhead. I blinked the grogginess from my eyes and the energy of the great tree washed over me.

Tait was staring around himself, alive with excitement.

"Have you been here before?" I asked him.

"To the tree, yes, once. But never to another Court."

"Why did you come here last time?"

Darkness swished over his features. "The king brought me here. He wanted to see if spinning shadows was more potent when done in such a sacred place."

Interest surged in me. "And? Was it?"

"No." Tait's usually relaxed face was tight. "It was extremely unpleasant and resulted in an unusable staff and significant damage to part of the sacred tree. I regret my actions that day enormously."

"Oh. I'm sorry."

His face cleared. "Prince Mazrith has no such greed-driven desires of my skills. This journey shall be entirely different," he beamed.

Yeah, this time you're likely to be attacked by undead creatures who want to eat you to get to me, I thought, but smiled back at him.

The giant tree trunk came into view and Mazrith joined us on the deck. A reverent quiet fell, the only sound the water lapping at the side of the boat as we approached the Shadow Court doors set into the trunk.

Mazrith gestured at Frima, and with a grateful smile, she lifted her staff. Hers had a scorpion tail at the top, and a purple gemstone. Shadows flowed from it, swishing into the braziers on either side of the gates, then flowing over the gruesome carvings. With a great creak, the doors swung open.

"How much earlier did the Queen leave than us?" I suddenly worried we'd run into her inside the tree if she had lingered.

"A few hours," Mazrith rumbled back as we sailed through the doors.

"Could she still be here?"

"I doubt it. No fae spends long inside the great tree of life."

"Why not?" We had moved inside, the doors closing behind us. I gaped around me at the serene, gentle lights, colossal white statues and soft green foliage.

"It becomes... uncomfortable."

Both the other fae gave him a look of agreement, but said nothing. I hoped the same wouldn't be true for Voror, as he was planning to spend as many days as we were in the Ice Court here.

On cue, the bird's voice entered my mind. "I am extremely comfortable in this place," he said. I glanced up as we moved gently past the statues, trying to spot him.

Hoping he wasn't too far away to hear me, I spoke. "Good luck, and stay safe."

Brynja shot me a look, and I gave her an awkward smile. "A prayer to the gods," I lied.

"There is nowhere safer. And I do not need luck. You, on the other hand, need all the gods will bestow," Voror replied.

I schooled my face, keeping my sarcastic smile at bay.

"I will see you shortly, Reyna," he said, his mental voice a touch softer than usual. "And I hope you have earned more braids when I do."

I smiled. He hadn't been around long, but he had been with me almost since my life got turned upside-down. I would miss him, even if it were only for a few days. A few days of life-threatening games designed to kill humans.

Too soon, we reached the huge doors to the Ice Court. As we approached, the braziers on each side leaped to life, burning a fiercely bright blue. With a creak, they eased open, revealing the root river on the other side.

I tensed, half expecting to be rushed by Starved Ones, but the waterway was empty.

How did the Starved Ones move between the Courts? The thought of them inside the tree felt utterly impossible.

The temperature was markedly cooler immediately after we passed through the gate, and the air no longer smelled of berries and earth, but of cool, crisp firs, despite there being no trees around us.

I moved to stand beside Mazrith, by the carved serpent figurehead. "Voror is staying behind in the tree," I said quietly. "He can't survive cold climates."

Mazrith looked at me with a flicker of concern. "He has helped you numerous times. It is a shame to lose his assistance."

"I agree. But he wants to have a look around for secret staircases while he's there." I shrugged. "He might be right and find something helpful."

The Prince's eyes bore into mine. "We must keep looking for another way."

"I agree. But I don't think making a new amulet is an option, unless you know a god to spell it for us when we're done."

He sighed. "You may be right."

"Any luck with learning to fly instead?"

He didn't roll his eyes, but the look he gave me meant the same thing, I was sure. "You can't just fly onto *Ravensstar island*."

"You say that like flying is easy."

"A mist-staff may give you the power," he muttered.

"Shame we have to do this first, in order to get one then." I stifled a yawn. "How long until we get to the Ice Court?"

"The stretch of river is long. Most of a day." I must have

reacted, because his face softened. "Sleep in the cabin a while. I wish to keep watch for enemies."

"I'll read first," I promised. His look told me he didn't believe me.

16

REYNA

I slept for a few hours in the warm bed, and when I woke to a knock on the door, there was no question we were nearing the Ice Court. I could see my breath in front of my face as I climbed reluctantly out of the furs. The door opened, and Frima stepped in, holding armfuls of more furs. She was clad in a black hooded cloak that clasped at the front with silver scorpion buttons.

"Here." She threw a fur at me, then left. I wasn't surprised when I saw that the buttons on the cloak she had given me were tiny owls, the same as my braid. I was surprised how much I liked them, though. When I was dressed and put the cloak on, I discovered it had deep pockets which had thick, fur-lined leather gloves in them, along with a thin, breathable scarf. I left the scarf in the pocket, donned the gloves, and went out onto the deck.

The sky above us was pale gray, the sides of the root-river lower than they had been before. Lumps of ice floated in the water as we sailed past, a soft thud every now and then when one hit the hull the only sound I could hear. Mazrith was still standing by the snake figurehead, talking with Tait.

Brynja bustled over with tea and a pastry held awkwardly in thick gloves.

"Thanks. Did you sleep well?"

"Fine, my Lady," she said unconvincingly. "The Gold Court has never experienced this temperature."

Her lips were pale, despite the thick furs she had on. "Go back in the cabin, we don't need anything else."

She opened her mouth to argue, then closed it and curtseyed. "Thank you, my Lady. Please fetch me if anyone needs anything."

"I will."

I went to join Mazrith and Tait. "How much farther?"

Tait was positively vibrating with energy. "Any moment now."

I had barely finished my tea before the root river opened up completely as we rounded a bend.

The icy water stretched as far as the eye could see, dotted with massive glaciers thirty feet high and wide, flat icebergs. The boat sailed through the narrow channels between the frozen islands, and I gazed up at the towering walls of blue ice as we passed them. Fat, round animals lay on icebergs, blinking thick-lashed black eyes at us in mild interest.

In the distance, I could see an immense ice palace carved into the side of an enormous glacier, with spires and turrets glittering in the pale light. I had to squint, my eyes so accustomed now to gloom. All three shadow-fae, and Tait, had pulled their hoods down low over their eyes, and I followed suit.

"Are we going to the palace?" I breathed.

"We're going where we are led," Mazrith said, pointing ahead. I leaned over the side to see that the icebergs were moving. The towering glaciers seemed to be fixed in place, but the large expanses of solid ice were shifting, forcing our boat down whatever path they chose.

Soon, our vessel glided through a channel into a secluded cove in the bottom of a bright blue glacier. A waterfall cascaded down from high up the glacier on our right, pouring into the cove, the spray creating fleeting rainbows in the air.

"It's beautiful," I breathed.

"Incredible," agreed Tait, voice awed.

"It's fucking cold," said Svangrior.

I gripped the side and saw a group of people on the shore of the cove, which was made from crystal clear ice. We thudded against it, and the boat stilled.

"Prince Mazrith of the Shadow Court," called an unfamiliar voice.

Mazrith pressed his mask onto his face, then vaulted over the side of the boat, onto the ice. Frima and Svangrior followed him. I looked at Tait.

"They don't want to see me." He smiled. "Off you go."

With a breath, and much more care than the others had taken, I climbed over the railings.

· · ·

I only had to drop a few feet onto the ice, but I stumbled on its slipperiness.

A group of grey-skinned, blue-haired fae in barely any clothing were standing before us, the male at the front holding a scroll. I looked behind them, seeing a tunnel carved in the ice, leading out of the cove.

The male spoke. "King and Queen Verglas welcome you for the *Leikmot*, but on hearing about the way Lady Kaldar and her kin were treated, are unwilling to host any visitors in his palace."

Mazrith, Frima and Svangrior exchanged looks.

"As such, we insist you reside on your ship for the duration of your stay. An honorary feasting hall has been erected to welcome you this evening."

"Thank you," said Mazrith, politely. "Where is the Shadow Court Queen and her contingent moored?"

The ice-fae barely concealed a lip curl. "Her fleet was large, so she has been offered a more sizeable cove. It is not safe in open ocean here. Ancient creatures roam the deep."

I let out a sigh of relief. At the same time, my brain created some terrifying sea monster images to add to my nightmares.

Not sharing a cove with the Queen was fine by me.

"And the other champions?" Mazrith asked.

"Lord Orm is a few glaciers to the west and Lord Dakkar the same to the east. You will be collected and escorted to the ball shortly."

Two females stepped out from behind him, pulling a barrel with them. "The King and Queen extend their hospitality to you."

They stepped back from the barrel. Mazrith frowned, but Tait called from the boat, "Thank you!"

All of the ice-fae glanced up at him and he waved enthusiastically. I was almost sure Mazrith's lips were twitching with amusement. The ice-fae gave one more bow of their collective heads, then as one turned and left through the tunnel.

"What's in the barrel, Tait?" called Frima.

"Liquid fire!"

Liquid fire turned out to be an oil very similar to the fuel in braziers in the Shadow Court, except it burned much hotter, and the warmth somehow spread much farther.

"What we use is based on this stuff, which was developed in the Fire Court," Tait said, bustling about the deck. "Back when trade was healthy between the Courts, ice-fae knew they had to keep visitors alive, so they learned to manufacture it themselves."

"Lucky for us," I said.

Strangely, the low-ceilinged cove and the warmth from the liquid fire created a kind of cozy setup.

Brynja, at least, had cheered up. "My Lady, we must get you ready for the ball."

I groaned. "I already stick out like a sore thumb. Can't I just go in my own clothes?"

"No," said Frima. "I'm about to put my dress on, you have to do the same."

I sighed and marched after Brynja to my cabin. I opened

the door and froze. Mazrith stood over an open chest, shirtless.

I was used to seeing his hulking form covered in fabric, and stared at how huge he still was under all the furs and armor. Huge and toned. And sculpted. And hard—

"Can you come back in a minute?"

His eyes swirled with shadows as I dragged my eyes from his solid stomach and blinked at him.

I didn't answer, just slammed the door closed. Brynja stared, wide-eyed at me. "We'll just wait here a minute." She nodded mutely.

Mazrith strode out a few minutes later in black fae robes adorned with silver, fine gloves, and boots that almost reached his thighs. "The cabin is all yours," he said. His voice seemed lower, huskier, and I avoided his gaze as I darted in.

I let out a long breath and sat down on the bed.

How could one naked chest make my heart flutter so bad?

Because you know how he could make you feel. The dream rushed my memories.

But that wasn't real. For all I knew, the real Mazrith was no good at pleasing a woman.

That notion lasted less than a heartbeat in my head. Every word he had said to me was real. His shadows were real. That huge, hard body was real.

"My Lady, here is your dress for tonight." Brynja dragged me from my thoughts by pulling something large and mostly blue from a chest and holding it up.

"Great," I said, without really looking.

She pooled it on the floor and directed me to step into it, then pulled it up and began to lace it up at the back. I looked down at the skirt and stilled.

"Fates, that's... That's beautiful."

It was made of a shimmering blue fabric that seemed to glimmer with its own light. Layers of sheer, gauzy fabric comprised the skirt, each layer a shade lighter than the one below, creating an ombre effect from midnight blue at the top to pale frost at the hem. Tiny crystals were embroidered onto each layer, so that when I swished it experimentally, it seemed as if stars themselves had been captured beneath the fabric.

"You look beautiful in it," she said. There was a small mirror above the basin in the corner, but it wasn't large enough to see the whole thing. I could see, though, that the strapless top plunged into a sweetheart neckline that offered a glimpse of more cleavage than I would have chosen.

Brynja handed me new gloves, made from delicate silver-blue silk that would run up to my elbows, and they too shimmered with a frosty glow.

It took her less time than usual to do my hair and makeup; I guessed because she was getting so much practice.

"You know, you could fit in with them, one day."

I frowned. "I'm not sure I want to. Although, I don't think the fae on this boat are our enemies." I gave her what I hoped was as reassuring look.

She didn't answer, but she did smile.

When I emerged onto the deck, the casual conversation

stuttered to a halt. Frima grinned at me, Svangrior glared, Tait nodded cheerfully, and Mazrith stared at me. Really stared.

"I thought you did not like gowns," he said when I reached them all at the table.

Brynja carried my cloak behind me, the warmth from the liquid fire enough that I could only just feel the prick of cold on my bare shoulders.

"I don't."

"Well, you sure as Odin wear them well," said Frima.

"Thanks."

Mazrith stood up abruptly. "I want to give you something," he said, clipped.

Frima snorted. "No doubt you do."

He glared at her, then marched into the cabin.

"I think you're supposed to follow him," Frima said in a mock whisper.

"Oh." With slight trepidation, I followed the Prince.

17

REYNA

The fact that Mazrith had all his clothes on when I entered filled me with a relief that fled when I met his face, replaced by searing heat and a desire to run and hide.

If I'd had any doubt that the fae Prince was attracted to me, it was gone now. Desire was etched into his features, his eyes firing with lust.

"I thought you said we couldn't—" I started, but he cut me off.

"Armor," he barked.

"W-what?"

"Your armor is ready."

I blinked, trying to stop picturing him crossing the space between us and crushing his lips to mine. "My armor?"

"Yes."

"I'm... I'm wearing a dress." I didn't know what else to

say, my flaming cheeks and heat filled core making my thoughts slow.

"I do not want you to go to the ball unarmed, so I wanted to give you these now." His voice was strained and he held out his hand. I took a tentative step forward, to see what he held.

They looked like silver talons, with strange metal rings behind them. I reached out and touched one and got a zing of heat though the silk gloves. I bit my lip to stifle a gasp. His pupils dilated at the small gesture, eyes dropping to my mouth.

"What are they?" I asked, breathless.

"They are finger talons. Designed especially for you."

He dropped all but one of the metal things onto the bed, then he took my pointer finger in his hand and slipped the talon over it. He pressed the little metal rings closed around my finger, and I stared. It was jointed, so that when I bent my finger, the talon bent with it, and the end looked razor sharp.

I looked up at him, his face still filled with heat.

"Do you like them?"

"Yes." I tried to calm my racing heart. "A bird of prey."

He nodded. "They are spelled so that they will not cut you. Just your foes."

"Thank you," I said.

Two different words were churning through my head though.

Over and over, like I was in a fog, and only half of what was happening was making it through the voice in my mind.

Kiss him.

Kiss him.

Kiss him.

I rose onto my tiptoes. His hands moved, grasping my waist, pulling me closer.

"This is not wise," Mazrith said roughly, even as his fingers tightened their grip.

"I know," I breathed. But my hands had moved of their own will, coming to rest against his chest, feeling his heart pound under my palms as I tilted my face up to his.

"We must not," he said, his voice ragged.

I didn't answer. I couldn't. The chanting in my mind drowned out all reason. My body moved of its own volition, driven by some instinctual need I couldn't deny.

Kiss him.

Kiss him.

Kiss him.

His fingers dug into the fabric of my gown. "We mustn't," he said again, but his protest was weak. His eyes dropped to my lips, which were now just a breath away from his.

I slid my hands up and around his neck, running my fingers through the soft hair at his nape. His grip on me tightened and a groan escaped his lips. The sound shattered what little restraint I had left.

I pressed my mouth to his, reveling in the sweet fire that raced through my veins at the contact. His lips moved against mine with a hunger that matched my own. The kiss deepened instantly, feverish and demanding. All thoughts of any consequences fled - there was only the way our bodies strained to meld into one.

Mazrith backed me against the wall, his body pinning me in place. I wrapped one leg around his hips, pulling him tighter against me. He groaned into my mouth, his hands roaming restlessly over my body, setting my skin aflame, leaving trails of heat in their wake. I gasped into his mouth as his fingers brushed the side of my breast through the stiff corset.

I was dizzy and breathless, lost to everything but the delicious feel of his hard body against mine, his lips and hands igniting my skin.

He broke the kiss abruptly and pressed his forehead against mine, his eyes, filled with swirling shadows, burning into me. I panted as I stared up at him. "We have to stop," he said, though he made no move to step away.

"I know," I said again. But my hands slipped under into the front of his robe, caressing the skin of his hard stomach. Heat pounded between my legs. With a growl, his lips found mine again. The kiss was rougher this time, edged with frustration and need. I reveled in it, craving his passion and the intense need in my core that bordered on pain.

"Do you have any idea what you do to me?" he murmured against my lips. *Yes.* I could feel him, hard and huge and ready, pressed against my body.

His hands slid lower, fingers running over my backside. "You will be the death of me, *gildi.*"

As he said the words, light sparked between us. We both froze, then watched as a gold rune floated from his cheek, followed by two more.

He stepped back, letting go of me as though I had burned him.

"What... why..." My words came out thick, my mind hazy with lust and confusion.

"We must stop," he said, roughly.

A loud knock on the door was followed by Frima's voice. "Erm, hate to interrupt you two, but the ice-fae escort is here."

Part of me was grateful for the interruption, but the rest of me screamed in protest. My body was alight with need, and my mind racing with questions.

Why did runes float from his skin? And why did it alarm him so much when it happened?

He leaned past me and pulled open the door, startling Frima on the other side. "We are coming." He closed it again and looked at me. "There are much larger things at stake than you and I. The fate of my Court, and maybe even *Yggdrasil,* if my stepmother is as twisted as I believe she is, are dependent on us finding that mist-staff." He swallowed, his eyes blazing. "We almost let our lust, and our tempers, set us back once. We must not give in to... superficial desires."

I wished the words didn't sting. Our desires *were* superficial. It wasn't like I loved him, for Odin's sake. It was my body that seemed so intent on our closeness.

Lies.

You respect him. And you've never respected anyone in your life like this before. I squashed the internal voice, and made myself speak. "You believe us being intimate would lead to us fighting?"

Again, his eyes flashed, and I knew there was more to it. "I believe the risk is not worth taking."

I held his gaze. He didn't lie. I believed his words — that us giving in to our passion was a risk. But he regularly omitted the truth.

I didn't believe the risk he was referring to was the one he had given me. There was more.

"They're getting annoyed, Maz! We need to go!"

With a growl of annoyance, he swept past me and opened the door, then paused. "The finger talons," he said, nodding at where the others lay on the bed. "Do not forget them."

"Mazrith, I—"

"We will talk. But not here, and not now."

I let out a breath as he left the cabin.

I hadn't known I was even capable of so many, and such intense feelings. The emotion, the confusion, the *desire*. All of it was too much.

But I had no time to work them out. I had to attend another fucking ball.

18

REYNA

We followed the two ice-fae sent to escort us through the tunnel in the glacier in silence. Once we were away from the heat of the brazier, the cold was biting, and I was grateful for my thick cloak. I had dropped the talons into the deep pocket, not trusting myself not to scratch or hurt the people around me until I had practiced wearing them.

When we emerged on the other side of the tunnel my breath caught. There was a central iceberg before us, surrounded by other glaciers I assumed hosted the other boats, and on it was a structure made entirely from ice. It was a smaller version of the palace I'd seen, I realized, gaping.

It glistened under the still pale twilight, its crystal spires reaching up toward the dusky blue sky. Walls of smooth ice blocks had been carved and fused together, reinforced by graceful arches everywhere I looked.

An intricate ice bridge, mercifully opaque, took us from the glacier to the iceberg, other fae visible as we approached the gardens surrounding it. Hedge mazes emerged from massive drifts of snow, bordered by ice sculptures of woodland animals and sea creatures. Frost-covered topiaries dotted the grounds, and a single weathered tree with silver leaves stood alone in a courtyard.

Tait was staring around in wonder as we approached the main entrance, a high open archway with no doors, and I thought Frima was struggling to keep the awe from her face as we climbed the glassy steps and entered the hall.

Frozen waterfalls tumbled down two curved walls, the ice transparent and flawlessly smooth. At the far end of the single room, an oval dais held two ice thrones, encrusted with gemstones and hoarfrost, a high and intricately carved arch over each.

Spiral staircases leading to a narrow balcony level wound up and down from the ballroom at intervals, each step a polished block of ice and the balustrades so fine they looked as though they would shatter with any pressure at all.

But the most eye-catching feature of the hall for me was the floor. It was made of a single slab of ice, clear and smooth, and beneath it was a great chasm, filled with icy water that glowed with an otherworldly light.

An answer to the blood-rivers under the throne room floor in the Shadow Court, perhaps? It made me uneasy, and I kept my gaze high, on the more beautiful features of the cavernous space.

An orchestra played chiming music from a balcony perched high above the gallery level, that echoed through the chamber and sounded almost eerie to me. Couples danced across the ice floor, gliding over its polished surface. The blue-haired females wore gowns of silvery silk and lace that blended with their pale skin, their faces hidden behind feathered masks of birds — mostly swans, ravens and doves. The males wore barely anything besides their masks, all the toned exposed flesh making my cheeks heat. Fur wraps around their middles and masks fashioned after foxes and wolves were all they seemed to need, even in the intense cold.

Magical lights flickered within the frozen waterfalls, throwing warm tones on the otherwise cool, twinkling light coming from the floor.

A thrall came over, his long brown hair tied back, and his body tightly wrapped in reddish-colored furs. He held up a tray covered in pink sparkling drinks.

I took one gratefully as Svangrior gave him a suspicious glare. I let out a hiss of surprise as the stemmed glass stung my skin through my gloves. The thrall gave me a knowing look.

"The glasses are ice, my Lady, and they melt fast," he whispered.

"Thanks for the tip."

Mazrith and Frima took one, and I sipped from the freezing vessel quickly.

"Fates, that's good," I breathed, surprised to find the glass empty when I lowered it. The glass was indeed disappearing under my numbing fingers. The thrall held a silver dish up, and everyone deposited their empty, melting glasses into it.

"I do not trust this place," Svangrior said, glaring after the thrall as he continued on to the next group of guests.

"You don't trust anyone," muttered Frima. Her gown was white and short, with a long lace trail at the back that gave it elegance. Her gaze lingered on the bare chests that surrounded us as she swatted him on the arm. "Loosen up, Svangrior. Have some fun." He scowled at her, then stomped off toward the tables groaning under the weight of bowls of food I mostly didn't recognize. She shrugged. "I meant something more exciting than food, but whatever." She looked at Mazrith. "Do you want to keep on eye on Tait, or shall I?" The shadow-spinner was already deep in conversation with two ice-fae women wearing huge swan masks.

Before Mazrith could answer her, a horn sounded, and all the chatter died as the music trailed neatly to a stop. Through the archway strode two fae who could only be the King and Queen of the Ice Court. King Verglas strode forth in a swirl of fur and steel, wearing a helm that glinted with a single, massive, diamond. His eyes were chips of pale citrine, cold and imperious, and his high cheek bones looked sharp enough to cut glass.

Queen Verglas glided, graceful at his side, her grey skin paler than any other ice-fae's in the room, and her hair a much whiter shade of blue too. Her spun-silver gown clung to her curves and strands of opal and moonstone were caught in her braids, pale as frost. Her eyes matched her husband's, just as hard and cold. I found her beauty intimidating, rather than appealing.

They ascended their thrones and a chill seemed to follow in their wake, stealing breath and warmth alike. King Verglas turned to survey the crowd of upturned faces. At his nod, flames leaped high along the walls of ice, but the fire was as blue as the glaciers outside.

"We bid you welcome." Queen Verglas raised her hands, long-nailed fingers glittering with rings of sapphires and diamonds. "The *Leikmot* has reached us. Let the celebrations commence!" At her words, music struck up again. The fae gave a cheer, many bowed, and then the dancing, eating, and talking resumed in earnest.

I scanned faces, looking for any I knew. Dakkar and the earth-fae were easy to spot, their skin tones so much darker than the ice-fae and gold-fae. The Shadow Court Queen stood out too, mostly due her obsidian black gown, and the height she had gained by piling her curls on top of her head.

She flashed a black-toothed smile at us and waved us over.

"I suppose we must play the part," I groaned.

"Rather you than me. I'll make sure Tait doesn't get himself kidnapped or killed," Frima said, then melted into the crowd after the *shadow-spinner*, leaving us alone. I looked at Mazrith, his eyes flashing behind the mask.

I dropped my voice. "You haven't said a word since we left the cabin. What is our plan?"

"No dancing," he growled.

My mind flashed to our dance at the first ball I had attended with him, and heat trickled through my veins. "No dancing," I agreed.

"We make polite conversation with my stepmother,

introduce ourselves formally to the King and Queen, then you speak with Dakkar."

I nodded. "Is there anything I should know about the ice-fae?" I asked as we began to walk toward Queen Andask and her minions.

"It is a little late to ask that, since we are now surrounded by them." I gave him a look, but at least I was getting more than clipped, one-word answers. "We know little about them, other than they have a love for gemstones, are formidable warriors and hunters, and take braids as trophies."

"Trophies?"

"From their kills."

"Oh."

"Tait can doubtless tell you more about them."

"This building is incredible. They obviously excel at ice architecture." I waved my hands, gesturing at the hall. He grunted. "You do not think so?"

"It is cold."

"Huh. Who could possibly like something both cold and beautiful?" I muttered.

He gave me a sharp look, but we had reached the Queen.

"Ah, my son!" she beamed.

"Stepmother," he answered stiffly.

Her courtiers were fanned around her, throwing narrow-eyed looks at me every time I glanced at them. I fixed my eyes on the Queen.

"And Reyna, how nice to see you. And you look so..." She gave me a long look up and down. "Delectable." She ran her tongue over her teeth, and I forced down my wave of revulsion.

I was aware of others looking and tried to force a smile.

Her own broadened. "I am keen to see what games the ice-fae have devised. Isn't it glorious than we are the first of our family to stand, invited, in another's Court in so many years?" She beamed at Mazrith.

"Glorious," he agreed, though his tone said there was nothing at all glorious about it. "Have a nice evening, stepmother."

He turned before she could reply, and I followed him with a rush of relief.

"Well, that was fairly painless," I muttered, swiping up another pink ice-glass from a passing thrall and downing the contents. "I thought we would have to endure her for longer than that."

"I have little patience this evening," Mazrith growled.

If he was even half has tightly wound as I felt, I didn't blame him for cutting his interaction with the Queen short.

"We must pay our respects to King and Queen Verglas."

I followed him to the back of a line of fae leading to the royals on their thrones. "How do you know the etiquette for visiting other Courts if you've never done it?"

"Tait reads. I read."

I tilted my head at him, but he wouldn't look at me. "Your mother wanted this," I remembered.

He looked sideways at me, shoulders dropping slightly. "Yes."

"Wouldn't she have wanted you to enjoy the experience, now you are here?" He glared at me, and I shrugged. "You can't deny that this place is beautiful." I gestured at the blue flames burning inside the frozen waterfalls, and the intricate balustrades. "Even if it is cold."

"Fine. It is... impressive. In its own way."

It didn't take us long to reach the thrones, and I copied Mazrith and bowed low to the seated royalty.

Neither the King nor Queen spoke to us, just bowed their heads in return, before a courtier waved us along to make room for the next guest.

"That's it?" I said as we walked along the far wall of the room, near the tables. "Not even a hello?"

"I am merely a Prince, and not worthy of conversing with. If tradition is upheld, then my stepmother should dine with them formally at some point during our stay. Are you hungry?" Mazrith asked me.

I nodded, though I suspected the hollow feeling in my gut was more to do with the lack of him between my thighs than an empty stomach. "I don't know what any of the food is though. I haven't seen it before."

"Wait here. I will get us something."

I watched his large dark form stride across the room to the food tables. Folk moved out of his way instinctively, his black robes and dark furs making him stand out before he got close to anyone.

"It is a shame you didn't get to visit the palace itself," a female voice said, making me jump in surprise and snap my eyes away from the Prince. A fae Lady had come over, wearing a turquoise peacock mask that stood out from most of the black and white ones.

"Oh, erm, yes, it is," I said, nodding. "Though this hall is very beautiful."

"You think so? Then you would have adored the palace." She looked at her friend, a man in a fox mask with about six silver rings through his bare nipples, then over at where Mazrith was standing at the tables, getting some food. I strongly suspected she was only talking to me because he wasn't there. "I think it's terrible, what Queen Andask did at the end of the Shadow Court games." Her voice held a scandalized tone.

"I agree," I said quietly.

She narrowed her eyes at me. "They say the Prince and Queen Andask do not always see eye to eye. That he disagreed with what she did too?"

"He did not approve," I said carefully.

She dropped her volume to a loud whisper. "Is it true that he was away fighting an invasion of the undead?" Her male friend leaned in.

"He was not in the palace at the time," was all I said.

She leaned back and huffed out a sigh through her nose.

"Appalling," she said. "You know, everything on these icebergs has been built especially for these games, far from the heart of the Court because of the untrustworthiness of shadow-fae. It's taken all the most powerful folk working solidly for days to get it all together." She tutted. "Poor Lady Kaldar."

Deciding that if she was going to fish for information, maybe I should too, I made my own tone conspiratorial. "Do you know what kind of games they have been working on?"

The fae looked down her angular nose at me, then her lips twitched into a smile. Slowly, she leaned back and stared at my hair. "I'll let you in on a little secret." She leaned forward, then whispered, "You don't belong here. In the games, in this hall, or even in *Yggdrasil*, with hair that color. Humans should be serving drinks or cooking our meals, or protecting our borders, not honored with fighting fae and marrying into royalty."

I breathed in hard through my nose and bit down on my tongue.

It was nothing I hadn't heard before. Except back then, I would have spat insults, knowing that as a *gold-giver* I would not be punished too severely because I was so valuable.

Here, I had no value. Even the Court I was representing wanted me to fail, didn't believe me worthy.

My hand rose, my fingers finding the end of my new braid in the hair that had drawn so much inexplicable hatred. The female's eyes followed my movement, and her male companion scoffed.

"Luck," he muttered.

Be worthy of the braid, Reyna. Honor. Dignity. That was what it symbolized.

Hurling insults at these fae wouldn't prove anything. Earning more braids, proving I was worthy? That would wipe the arrogance from their faces.

"Humans should not be underestimated," I said, lifting my chin. "And a person's hair color says nothing about their honor or courage." Lhoris had told me that so many times when I had been a raging teenager.

Mazrith strode into view before she could answer, and I

reached for the plate he handed me gratefully. The female gave him a lightning-fast bow, then scurried off, the fox-masked male hurrying after her.

"Looking for gossip," I told him at his questioning look, moving my gaze to the plate instead of his piercing irises. "Now, what are we eating?"

19

REYNA

"I really don't think he'll tell me anything," I mumbled, as Mazrith walked me across the now heaving dancefloor toward Dakkar and his group of earth-fae. "He's my competitor."

Huge skirts twirled on each side of us, and I wished we could join the dancers so I could feel Mazrith's strong arms around me, instead of having to talk to more fae who thought I was pathetic.

"We should not pass up this opportunity to find out more about my stepmother's plans." Mazrith answered inside my head, but when I turned to scowl at him, he had vanished into the crowd.

I sighed and forced myself to move on.

When I reached Dakkar, the group of earth-fae fell silent. Most regarded me coolly, but Dakkar grinned.

"Gold-giver," he greeted me. "Ready for more games tomorrow?"

"They can't be worse than what Queen Andask planned," I answered. I looked for the two fae who had been strung up in the throne room, but didn't see them amongst the group. A thrall came by with more glasses, and I took one and drained it. "How are the folk she took from you doing?"

Dakkar's smile faltered. "Recovered. I do believe though that my own King will do as the Ice Court has, when our turn comes. There will be no warm welcome into the heart of our Court."

I nodded. "I understand that. Do you know why Queen Andask planned the *Leikmot* in the first place?"

He frowned at me. "To celebrate her son's birthday."

"He's not her son," I said automatically.

Dakkar cocked his head at me. Everyone in his group was listening intently to our conversation, and I struggled not to look at them all. "Your presence, not just in these games, but in the Shadow Court, is most intriguing," the earth-fae said.

"For you and me both. But Prince Mazrith has nothing to do with these games, and truth be told," I leaned in conspiratorially, "he has little love for his stepmother."

Dakkar eyed me. "He looked angry about the stunt she pulled after the games," he said eventually.

"He has honor."

"You would say that. You are his betrothed."

"Not by choice," I said, and for some reason, felt a pang of guilt for saying so.

"Really?" Dakkar stepped closer to me, interested. "We do not force marriage in our Court, but many find

147

ways to take what they want." Darkness crossed his green eyes.

I waved my hand. "I don't think they force marriage in the Shadow Court either. Our situation is kind of complicated." I seized on the opportunity to bring up Orm. "They do have forced marriage and concubine-binding in the Gold Court though."

Dakkar snarled. "The Gold Court is driven by greed and lust."

"You dislike Lord Orm?"

"There is little to like about him."

"Do you... Do you think he knew about the Queen taking our loved ones before it happened?"

Dakkar stilled. "Why do you ask that?"

"He didn't look as surprised, or concerned, as you and Lady Kaldar."

"He wasn't concerned because one of his most precious things was a fucking golden trinket," Dakkar snorted.

I shrugged. "I just wondered if there was something between the two of them."

Dakkar's eyebrows rose. "Between a shadow-fae queen and gold-fae lord?" His finger went to his lip. "But then, I'm speaking to a *gold-giver* human betrothed to a shadow-fae prince. So I suppose anything is possible." He regarded me a moment longer. "I do not know anything about why your Queen orchestrated the *Leikmot*. We received an invitation, and the rulers of my Court deemed it worth regarding."

"And what made them trust her?"

A few fae behind him laughed. "Oh, little human. We do

not trust her. But we can't learn any more about our rivals from behind our own bark."

Somehow Dakkar called me a little human in a much less condescending way than when others did it. He was almost seven feet tall, so to be fair, I *was* little. "So you're here to find out what she is up to?"

"As, it appears, are you."

"I wish that *was* why I was here," I muttered. I looked into his face, trying to project honesty. "I'm fairly sure the point of these games is to kill me."

"Then she may end up satisfied." I scowled at him and he grinned. "Nice braid, by the way."

My scowl slipped away. "Thanks."

Dakkar glanced over my shoulder. "Enjoy the ball, and see you in the games tomorrow." He turned his back to me, the conversation clearly over.

I turned, expecting to see Mazrith. Instead, Orm was gliding smoothly in my direction, his eyes glinting behind his golden mask. "A dance, I think," he purred when he reached me, grasping my arm. His touch sent a shudder through me, and I tried to pull away, but he dragged me toward the dancing fae.

Turning me, he grabbed at my other hand, his fingers tightening painfully as he awkwardly twirled me around. I tried to stay calm, to not let him know he was rattling me. But being anywhere near him made my stomach turn. "It has been hard to catch you alone. You don't belong here, little human," he growled under his breath, lowering his head toward mine. I sucked in a hiss as he squeezed my arm even harder. "You belong in my bed, naked, bound, and ready for me whenever I want you."

Fury flooded through me, and I yanked my hand from his, diving it into my pocket. I slammed my foot down onto his, grinding hard as I stabbed one silver talon deep into his wrist. Orm yelped, releasing me, then snarled in fury. He raised one hand, clearly to hit me, his other going to the staff at his belt. I took a stumbling step backward and hit something hard.

Mazrith.

His shadows tumbled around me, and I pressed myself harder into his chest, my heart racing. Orm's furious expression flickered as he looked from my face up into Mazrith's.

Slowly, he lowered the hand he had been about to hit me with but kept his other on his staff. "You wish to marry her?" he said. "A filthy freak?"

Mazrith growled, more animal than fae, no words discernible in the raw sound.

Orm's face twisted in an answering snarl, and scarlet blood from the wound I'd made on his wrist bloomed on his white robes, his flashing eyes fixed on me. "I will see you tomorrow, without your guard-hound." He whirled away.

I turned slowly. Mazrith was still as hard as rock, his jaw twitching as he watched Orm move across the hall.

"I had it covered," I said quietly. I didn't know if I would have been fast enough to duck the blow Orm had been about to throw, but drawing blood was sure-as-Odin satisfying.

Mazrith didn't look at me, his eyes still fixed on Orm's

retreating figure. Another growl sounded in his chest though.

"The talons work." This time his eyes flicked down to mine.

"I will do more than make that bastard bleed," he rasped.

I laid one hand tentatively on his chest, trying to breathe though the jolt of energy I felt with the contact. His hard chest somehow stiffened even more. "If you could help *me* do more than make him bleed, I'd be grateful."

His hulking shoulders dropped a tiny bit, the vein working in his neck settling as he stared at me. "He is *your* enemy. Not mine." It was a statement, rather than a question.

An out-loud realization, perhaps.

I nodded. "Twice now, I have been able to stand up to a fae Lord who has abused countless human women in my home. I owe it to them, as well as myself, to be the one who ensures he never hurts another."

Understanding was written all over Mazrith's stony face. "You will be the one who ensures his manhood never feels anything again but the touch of steel. I will ensure it."

"Thank you." Cold fury still danced through his eyes, and I was keenly reminded that the male I was standing before was known to the world as a monster. "You're not actually expecting me to cut his dick off, are you?" I whispered.

"Males like him do not deserve one."

"I agree, but, honestly, that's not my style. Plus, I don't want to go anywhere near his dick."

Mazrith tensed again, more flashing anger in his face. He started to speak, but I pressed my hand harder against his chest and cut him off. "I made him bleed on his nice white robes, so let's call that a victory for tonight and see what comes tomorrow, in the games."

My heart kept jumping into my throat as we made our way back to the glacier that hosted our cove and boat, and not because of the altercation with Orm. The gold-fae Lord had returned to the ball in fresh white robes, minus the blood stain, but hadn't come anywhere near either of us again. That hadn't stopped Mazrith from remaining tense and stiff for the rest of the evening, eyes constantly scanning for threats and landing on Orm.

His fierce protectiveness over me had made my stomach flutter before, and tonight had been no different.

But that wasn't what was making my heart skip. He'd been there for me, but just like in the alley in Slaithwaite, he had agreed to let me own my own battle. He respected me in a way that nobody ever had before, and he had a faith in my strength that I never would have believed a fae could give a human. *Or whatever the fates I was.*

He believed I could best Orm. And he would be there to rip his head, or dick, off if I couldn't. The feeling that gave me was so unfamiliar, and so fucking good, it almost made me giddy.

But it also made it increasingly difficult to pretend my attraction to him was simply physical.

. . .

When we got onto the boat, Mazrith swept straight to Frima and Brynja's cabin, rapping on the door. A sleepy Brynja poked her head out, hair disheveled, then squeaked as she saw Mazrith's glowering face.

"You are moving to Tait's cabin. Now."

She nodded quickly, then backed into the cabin.

Frima sauntered up next to me. "So, you two had a bad night then," she muttered.

Mazrith turned back to us. "Frima, in with Reyna. If anyone enters that room, fight first, ask questions later."

"Whatever you say, Maz," she said, then moved toward her cabin.

Svangrior sighed and made his way to his own room. "Tait, I'm moving out, Brynja's moving in," he said as he opened the door.

Mazrith and I were left standing on the deck, staring at each other.

"Don't want to share with me, huh?" I said quietly.

He closed the gap between us with startling speed, and a small gasp escaped me as he gripped my chin, tipping my face up to his. "I know when I can trust myself, and when I cannot," he rasped. His eyes dropped, raking over my body, his forearms tensing. "Tonight, I cannot."

"Would it be so bad?" I whispered, all the unfulfilled need from earlier pounding back through my body.

"The risk is too great," he ground out.

Frustration made me narrow my eyes. "You are not being truthful about what we would be risking."

He stilled, staring. "No," he admitted eventually. There was movement behind him, and I could hear Tait muttering.

"Is that fair?" I said, as quietly as I could.

"Nothing in *Yggdrasil* is fair anymore," he snarled. I thought he was about to do his signature whirling away move, but he paused. He took my arm at the elbow, releasing my chin. My breath caught as he lifted my forearm.

Painfully gently, he lowered his head and kissed my wrist, exactly where the runes were etched into my skin beneath my silk glove.

Desire so powerful it almost had me seizing his head in my hands coursed through me. But he was gone before I could say a word, disappearing into the cabin Brynja had just left.

Frima stood in the doorway of my cabin, shaking her head at me. "Freya help me, you two are a mess."

20

REYNA

I found myself pleased that it was Frima who helped with my new armor the next morning. Mazrith being that close to my body would mess with my head, and I needed to be able to think clearly. And I had come to associate Frima with fighting and skill, which was exactly what I needed before the first game at the Ice Court.

"How's that?" she asked, looking me up and down. I rolled my shoulders, amazed at how light the metal feathers were, and how well they moved with my body.

"Good." There were sheaths for my thighs in long, light strips, decorated with curved feather designs, and I had my finger talons on over black leather gloves. My hair was tied back, my headband now a standard part of my daily wear, and I had agreed to two thin zigzag stripes of navy paint on my cheeks.

"Then let's go."

When we emerged onto the deck our ice-fae escorts

were waiting. Mazrith had insisted that Tait stay on the boat this time, so the four of us followed them through the tunnel through the glacier once more.

A boat was waiting, the bridge and the ice structure from the night before gone, an empty iceberg in its place.

The peacock fae-Lady hadn't been lying when she said the landscape shifted, I thought.

The *karve* we traveled in had a beautifully carved whale figurehead, and it moved quickly through the channels in the ice until we reached a large iceberg covered with packed snow and an icy forest, dark firs poking out of heaps of white powder.

The boat stopped by rows and rows of benches made from ice, hosting the spectating fae. The King and Queen were in thrones at the head of the viewing area, and I could see Queen Andask, surrounded by her shadow-fae.

Orm, Dakkar, and Kaldar were arriving in boats too, and the crowd clapped as we all made our way onto the iceberg.

"Welcome to the first game in the Ice Court round of the *Leikmot*," said the King, his voice magically magnified. "This will be a test of both wit and strength." My stomach squished nervously as I glanced around for clues. Wit, I might stand a chance, strength, much less so. "I will give you no instruction, save to say that if your repairs are not made in time, you do not want to remain inside."

I scowled. What did that mean?

In response to a movement from his staff, the snow-covered trees parted, a path clearing in the forest, leading to four small structures. Half the size of the cabins on the boat, they looked to be made of blocks of ice stacked upon each other. "Enter," the King said. The other three fae began walking down the path towards the buildings. With a last glance back at Mazrith and Frima, I followed them.

There was a rune over each of the open entrances into the buildings. Runes for gold, earth, ice and shadow. I moved to the shadow rune building, distinctly aware of how wrong it was that I could possibly be representing the Shadow Court.

There was a loud gong sound as we all cautiously entered our buildings. Gloom rushed me as the door immediately sealed over with icy blocks.

I moved, banging against the ice in panic, and the ground rumbled beneath me. A creaking sounded, and I froze.

If your repairs are not made in time, you do not want to remain inside.

That was what the king had said. My eyes were adjusting to the change in light from the bright, pale outside, the ice transparent enough that a blueish light filtered through.

There was another huge rumble and more creaking, and then huge blocks were tumbling from the walls into the empty space.

I dodged and skipped out of the way as they fell, my heart pounding as the shuddering and collapsing came to a stop.

"Commence the repairs! First out wins," boomed the king's voice.

Catching my breath, I looked around. Light beamed in

through six holes, and six huge blocks lay on the snow-covered ground.

Worry washed through me. The highest hole was a foot above my head, and the blocks looked far too heavy for me to lift that high. The others, with their magic, would have far less problem lifting things.

I crouched to pick up a block and move it to the nearest, lowest hole.

It was freezing cold, even through my gloves, and it weighed as much as I feared it would. I dragged it over to a hole on just the second row of blocks and heaved it up and into place. Ice slid against ice satisfyingly. I turned, ready to get the next block, but there was a cracking sound, and then the block flew from its hole, smashing into the opposite wall. The whole building creaked and wobbled and I held my breath.

Why the fates had it spat the block back out?

I leaned over, looking for anything on the square hole that might have stopped it staying put. A rune was carved into the bottom, shining blue. *Black.*

I rushed over to the block, checking for any markings. *Water.*

What did that mean? I checked the other blocks, having to turn them to check all the sides, until I found the runes on each one.

Figure, River, Night, Path and *Pitch.*

I went through all the words in my head, pairing them with *Black*, then hauled the *Pitch* block over, my back protesting as I hefted it up onto my knees, then slotted into the hole.

I moved out of the way fast, in case it was going to launch the block back out again.

It didn't.

Nodding in satisfaction, and buoyed by my small success in solving the puzzle, I moved to the next hole, two rows higher and a way to the left. *Way*.

That could match *Water*, or *Path*. Picking the nearest of the two, *Water*, I pushed it along the ground, then lifted it. My arms ached as I lifted it awkwardly to shoulder height, then shoved it into the hole. I had barely pushed it all the way in before the creaking sounded, and I wasn't fast enough. It hit me on the shoulder as it was forcefully ejected, and the rumble in the ground was so strong I fell onto my knees, throwing my hands out to steady myself. More creaking and cracking came from the ceiling above me, and I glanced up. How many errors could I make before the building came down on top of me?

I selected the other block, pushing it over, then once again summoning my strength to lift into the hole. This time, it stayed put.

Not wanting to make any more mistakes, I decided to check the other four holes and match them to their pairs before wasting energy, and errors, moving blocks.

Head, Sky, Mouth and one rune I did not recognize. Remembering with a jolt that Dakkar couldn't read, I felt a pang of concern for the earth-fae and a surge of gratitude for Kara.

The ones I knew, I felt confident of the matches. *Figure* went with *Head*, *River* with *Mouth* and *Night* with *Sky*. Assuming that those three matched, then I could figure the fourth one by process of elimination. I set about trying to get the other blocks into their holes.

Not believing for a moment I could do this faster than the others, I wondered what the spectators would be doing outside. Surely this would be boring for them?

As if reading my thoughts, I saw a flash of light move above me as I pulled a block across the snow. I glanced up just in time to see the ceiling flash into a solid glass plate, like a mirror. But, instead of my reflection in it, I could see the crowd, the King and Queen in their thrones, and the groups of visiting fae watching on. Almost as soon as I had seen it, it vanished again, leaving me no time to look for Mazrith.

So they were watching through some magical mirror?

Huffing annoyance that I was being watched without realizing it, I redoubled my efforts with the block.

The next two blocks went into their holes without being rejected, and I was surprised the game hadn't already ended. Surely one of the others had magicked all the blocks into place by now?

I had pretty much given up on winning as soon as I'd felt the weight of the ice, and was just pleased that I wasn't anywhere near Orm, or anything else that would kill me. Save for the building collapsing on me. Did we have to finish the task to be allowed out?

I looked up nervously at the highest hole. I would have to get the block above my head to get it in, something I wasn't sure my human strength would allow.

As I pulled the fifth block over to its corresponding hole,

the ground shuddered, and the King's voice rang out. "The first fae has completed the task!"

A weird relief rolled through me. I wouldn't have been able to lift the last block anyway. I turned to the blocked door, hoping it wasn't Orm who had won.

"The order in which the rest of you finish will decide the advantages for a future game. Play on!"

"Horseshit," I cursed loudly, sending a glare up at the ceiling.

Before I could even crouch to pick up the next block, the ground rumbled again and the whole building shifted around me. "Hey!" I hadn't made another mistake, so why was my building shaking?

Waiting for it to stop so that I could lift my block, I steadied myself with my hand on the hole. When I touched it, though, the shaking got more vigorous. I tried to grip it for balance, my gloves sliding on the ice and refusing me purchase. Snapping sounds joined the creaking, and I felt my stomach drop. A huge crack snaked its way across the ceiling. Blocks shook themselves loose as I watched in horror, no idea what to do to stop the shaking.

This thing was coming down. With me in it.

21

REYNA

I hurled myself to the ground, getting as close to one of the blocks as I could, but I knew it couldn't offer me any protection. A clash and the sound of smashing had me throwing my arms over my head. The ceiling was coming down. I tried to crawl and tipped sideways, rolling out of the way of huge lumps of ice.

Panic scrambled my mind, the bangs and crashes deafening in the space. I hit the side of the building and straightened, lunging for the hole I hadn't yet filled. I was sure I couldn't fit through, but I had nothing else to try. I grabbed the hole, and the side of the building shuddered, then leaned ominously. Time seemed to slow as the blocks of ice at the top teetered, then began to slide toward me.

A bright white light seared my eyes, and I cried out, throwing my arm across my face. Heat warmed the air across me, and I gasped as freezing cold water tumbled over me. I moved my arm, panting in confusion.

Orm. Orm was standing where the wall was, the whole building reduced to a puddle of water.

Light rushed back to his staff, illuminating the cruel sneer on his face.

"What- why-" I gasped for breath, the air bitingly cold on my wet clothes and skin.

"I do believe you were about to become a casualty of the *Leikmot*," Orm said quietly.

I looked around at the melted building, then back to him. "You melted the ice? Why?"

He smiled. "You are deaf? Or stupid? I told you already. I do not wish you dead. My tastes run to the eclectic, I grant you, but necrophilia is not one of them."

My stomach roiled. "You saved my life just to be able to take me as your own later?"

"Yes. But I'll get so much more from it than that. You owe me a debt now, little human. Your life."

"I do not owe you my life," I spat. The words, filled with as much venom as I could muster, did not ring true. I would have been crushed to death if he'd not shown up.

A gong sounded, then feet were pounding on snow. I turned, still drenched, and saw fae running down the path through the forest, Mazrith and a brown-skinned earth-fae at their head.

Kaldar was leaning against her intact building, the doorway open, but the building beyond her was completely collapsed. The earth-fae ran straight to it with inhuman speed, just as a cocoon of leafy vines burst through the pile of ice-bricks, a hand sticking out of them. Dakkar had managed to shield himself, I realized with a jolt of relief.

"Reyna." I turned to Mazrith as he reached us. After a quick glance over me, he snapped his head to Orm. "Why?" he barked.

"To see your face when you admit that your betrothed owes me her life," he hissed.

I willed Mazrith not to react. Not to give him the satisfaction. His neck was so tight the veins bulged, and lethal fury swirled in his eyes as shadows flurried from the top of his staff. But they moved to me, not Orm. They did nothing when they reached me, just swirled around me.

Mazrith spoke loudly enough for those nearby to hear him. "Very honorable of you, Lord Orm. I thank you. You will be a guest of honor at our wedding."

Orm's smile slipped. "You will be my guest of honor, when I get what I want from that pathetic, broken little girl," he hissed. "That is why I kept her alive. For you to witness the pleasures you are trying to take from me."

I stepped forward before Mazrith could say anything, copying his overly loud tone. "You are right, I do need to leave now and warm up. Thank you again." I forced myself to bow my head, and turned, moving so fast back down the path I was almost jogging. The shadows came with me.

Frima was ten feet away and fell into step beside me. "Is Mazrith coming?" I asked, without turning.

"Yes. He tried to get to you before but the King wouldn't let anyone interfere."

I nodded. "Why did the building come down? Was it deliberate? Did I run out of time?"

"I don't know, the King and Queen looked surprised.

But, they did nothing about it. Yours and Dakkar's collapsed as soon as Kaldar got out."

We had reached the spectators, and the Ice Court royalty watched me as I made my way straight to the *karve* with the whale figurehead. With a wave of her hand, the Queen sent two escorts to the boat. I climbed in. Frima, then Mazrith and Svangrior followed.

Without a word, Mazrith shrugged out of his massive fur cloak. He pulled my soaking wet one off, and replaced it, the expanse of material swamping me. It was warm from his body, and I didn't keep in my sigh of relief at the respite from the cold.

"Thank you."

"Do not thank me," he ground out as the boat pushed off from the iceberg.

"It wasn't your fault, Maz," said Frima. He glared at her, then at the back of our escorts. He was clearly not going to speak about it in company. I pulled his fur cloak tighter around myself and sent a prayer to Freya that he had some of that burning drink on the boat.

Brynja and Tait were on the deck when we got back to the ship, the brazier kicking out welcome warmth. When the maid saw Mazrith's thunderous face she leaped to her feet and rushed toward the cabin.

"Brynja, nettle wine and brandy," called Frima after her. The girl squeaked her acknowledgment.

I made my way straight to my cabin to remove my wet

clothes. Frima came with me, and I frowned as she stepped into the cabin.

"Armor," she said. "Unless this is like the dress thing, and you want to try and do it yourself?"

I shook my head. "No. I'd appreciate the help."

I dropped Mazrith's cloak and she helped me out of the armor. "Shame it didn't help," I mumbled, admiring the shine as I laid it out carefully in one of the open chests. It had dried instantly, the water not clinging to the metal like it had my clothes. The fabric of my trousers and shirt had started to freeze, stiff and unwieldy against my tingling skin.

Frima blew out a sigh. "Why did Orm save you?"

"He said because he wanted me, and Maz, to owe him."

Frima's face twisted into a snarl. "That's fucked up."

I nodded. "He's fucked up." Hesitantly, I told her about some of the stories I'd heard about him and his concubines as I removed my frozen garments and replaced them with a thick woolen green dress, and rubbed a fur blanket over my cold, wet hair.

"And... he chose you to be bound to him next?"

"Yes. I was planning to leave the Gold Court the night you came."

Frima stared at me a while, eyes thoughtful.

"What?" I asked her, shrugging. "You're going to tell me I wouldn't have survived the other courts, because I'm a *gold-giver*?"

"No."

"Really?"

"I'm inclined to believe you would have survived. You'd have been fucking miserable though. And very, very lonely."

"Better lonely than the plaything of Lord Orm."

"I agree. And despite his reasons, I'm glad he did save you. Come. Let's get you some brandy."

22

REYNA

azrith was at the head of the ship when we came back out on deck, staring out at the frozen sea beyond the cove. Brynja handed me a glass when I sat down at the table and I took it gratefully.

"What happened?" Tait said in a loud whisper. "The Prince seems very angry."

Frima gave him a shortened version.

"The next game is tomorrow," grunted Svangrior. "You may do better then."

I nodded, relieved that it wasn't today. As much as I knew we had to get back to the Shadow Court, I didn't feel like seeing Orm's face again so soon.

"I overheard some fae talking," the warrior continued. "Ice-fae courtiers of the royals, and I'm sure they said something about the next game having to do with water."

I raised my eyebrows, and Mazrith turned from the snake figurehead. He walked slowly toward us. I held out his cloak to give back to him, but he didn't take it. Mine was still wet, Brynja busily hanging all my wet clothes over the rails near the brazier, so I wrapped it back around my shoulders, still cold enough from the soaking I got to feel the biting frost through the brazier's warmth.

"Water?" Mazrith said to Svangrior.

He nodded. "I caught one say something like, *all fae should be able to swim, but I wonder if humans are taught.*"

All heads turned to me. "Can you swim?" Frima asked me.

"A little. When I was younger." I hadn't exactly had lessons or much practice, but I had snuck down to the palace fountains as a child, knowing that's where the other kids in the palace played. They hadn't let me join them, so I started going on my own, trying to teach myself to spite them. I hadn't shown a natural aptitude and had given up quickly.

Mazrith's tense gaze fixed on me. "We will find somewhere to practice. Now. Drowning is not pleasant."

I swallowed. "Where? I'm not getting in that." I pointed past the boat to the ice-filled water. "Fates, please don't tell me they're going to make us swim in freezing water? Humans die really, really fast in freezing water." I was struggling to keep the panic from my voice.

Tait spoke. "No, no, all fae except ice-fae will die quickly in freezing water. That would be poor taste indeed, creating a game geared solely for the hosting court."

I gave him a look. "I'm human in a bunch of games designed for beings with magic."

"You're sort of an exception. Anyway, no, this Court has hot springs."

"Hot springs?"

He leaned over the many books scattered across the tabletop. "Aha." He picked one up and flicked through the pages, before turning it around to show us. "Hot springs."

There was a drawing of a glacier with a lake in the bottom, like a pool. Steam seemed to drift from its surface.

"Why would ice-fae want somewhere hot to go?"

"The same reason we have hot and cold places," Tait shrugged. "And the Courts weren't originally designed by the gods to only host one type of fae. War and discord between us was not the plan."

"That's why the Shadow Court isn't even darker than it is," Mazrith said quietly. He looked Tait. "Are there many of these hot springs?"

Tait nodded. "Yes, this is a large Court, compared to our mountain. It is most fascinating."

Mazrith strode to the railings, then vaulted over, onto the ice. I heard him call out, then two guards appeared in the tunnel, wearing shining white armor and holding their staffs high.

He spoke with them a moment, then climbed back onto the boat. "I asked if we may visit a hot spring for you to warm up. They said they will check with their chief."

I had barely finished my brandy before a voice called up to us, across our cove. "We shall escort you to the nearest spring."

Mazrith and I followed the ice-fae in silence. My nerves were jangling. I had hoped Frima would be helping me practice swimming, but Mazrith had told the others to stay on the boat and keep private conversations to the cabins.

I didn't know what one was supposed to wear when swimming, but as a kid, it had always just been my undergarments. That really didn't feel like a smart idea with the Prince.

We didn't go far, just through the tunnel to the other side of the glacier. Instead of getting in a boat, the ice-fae took us right, along an alarmingly narrow ledge in the bright blue glacier that I wouldn't have even noticed. About ten feet along, she paused, lifted her staff, and tapped it on the ice. There was a cracking sound that instantly set me on edge, then a chunk of the ice slid back to make an entrance.

She walked in and we followed.

"Wow." We were in another cove, presumably right next to the one our boat was in, except much smaller, the opening leading out onto the sea barely big enough to admit a vessel. It was warmer in this cove too, the steam rising from the surface of the pool of water in front of us making the air moist.

"These are guest glaciers," the ice-fae said, looking at me as I breathed my admiration. "They all have hot springs, boat shores, and..." She trailed off. Apparently, we hadn't yet earned whatever else the guest glaciers had to offer.

"Will you leave us, please?" Mazrith asked, looking at her. "I wish to spend some time alone with my betrothed." My pulse quickened.

The flash of curiosity on the fae's face was quickly replaced with the practiced nonchalance of a guard. "I will be at my post by the tunnel." She nodded her head, then left the cove.

Mazrith watched her leave. "She does not disapprove of a human and a fae being together," he said quietly.

"How do you know?"

"I read people well."

I pulled a face. "Their minds?"

He moved his gaze to me. "That has helped hone my skills, but no. I didn't read her mind. I can tell."

"Huh."

"The same way I can tell there is more to Lord Orm and his part in all this than we are aware of."

I took a breath, the warm air pleasant. "You think there is another reason he kept me alive?"

"Perhaps."

"He can't know about the mist-staff, can he? That's the only reason I can think of that he would need me alive."

"Aside from the pleasure of tormenting you?"

"Yes. Aside from that."

"No," Mazrith shook his head. "I don't see how he can know about the mist-staff, or your role in finding it. My mother searched for years, with guidance she never confided in me."

Guidance? The same guidance Voror had received? The mysterious fae maybe?

"Then, I guess Orm is just twisted enough to have saved me to spite us. I mean, much as I hate to admit it... I'm glad he did."

Rage fired in Mazrith's eyes. "I couldn't get through the Ice Court King's barrier. Reinforced with his wife's magic, they are stronger than I am."

"I know you'd have saved me if you could have."

"With a mist-staff, I would be powerful enough."

I put my hand on his bulging arm as his fists clenched around his staff. "Maz, let it go. I'm alive. And you're about to help me learn to survive the next game."

He stilled, the rage draining from his eyes. "Maz. You called me Maz."

"Hm. That's the second time I've done that. It's being around your friends so much."

With an abrupt move, he spun away from me and leaned his staff against an angular boulder of ice. He pulled his shirt over his head, and I blinked thickly at his huge bare shoulders.

"Do not get in that water naked, or I will not be responsible for the outcome," he growled, before yanking off his boots, then trousers.

"Why do you get to be naked?" I stuttered, staring transfixed at his backside. His powerful legs moved, and he slipped quickly into the spring, the steamy surface covering his bare skin and allowing me to breathe again.

"I have no undergarments." He still had his back to me as he moved through the pool. "There are steps down," he said. "Be careful."

"You don't wear underclothes?" Were men supposed to wear something under their trousers? Having only ever lived with one male, Lhoris, and having never been anywhere near his clothing, I had never considered it before.

"Tell me when you are in the water," he said, his back still to me.

"This is a bad idea," I mumbled, shrugging out of Mazrith's cloak and setting it down with his clothes.

Or a fucking fantastic idea. He was naked. In real life, not a dream.

My stomach was swooping as I unlaced the simple fastening on my dress, and heat pricked at me in all the right places. I had a knee-length shift with thin straps on under my dress, and plain cotton underwear beneath that. I was fairly sure the material would be see-through when wet.

My breath hitching, I moved to the side of the pool, first sitting on the edge and putting my bare feet in. The water was deliciously warm. Slowly, I slid in the rest of the way, my feet searching out the steps Mazrith had mentioned. As soon as the shift got wet, it clung to my skin.

"I'm in," I told Mazrith, once my breasts were under the water and out of sight.

"Good. When was the last time you swam?"

"Erm, ten years ago?"

He turned, eyes scanning my face, then my bare shoulders. "Move off the step, see if you remember."

I went to do as he asked, but hesitated. "You won't let me drown?"

He moved closer to me, water up to his solid pecs. "I'm standing on the bottom. It is not deep enough to drown."

"Oh," I said, relieved. I pushed off the step, letting the water take my weight and kicking with my feet. My arms flailed, and my head went under. I found the bottom,

174

COURT OF MONSTERS AND MALICE

pushing myself back up and gasping. The pool was deep enough that my chin was still under the surface.

"Fates," I gasped, pushing my hair back from my face. "Why didn't you catch me?"

Mazrith stared at me. "You were under less than a second."

"Oh. It felt like longer." The strap of my shift stuck to me as I lifted my arm higher to try to move more of my hair back.

"Go back to the step. Try again."

Mazrith watched me as I tried to get some sort of balance in the water. Most of what I gave him was clumsy, splashy, flailing.

"Watch me," he said eventually. He moved to the step beside me, his chest rising from the water. I gulped. Now he was naked and wet. How in the name of Freya was I supposed to concentrate with his bare skin glistening in front of me?

He pushed off the step, gliding through the water, powerful limbs slicing through the surface. I tried not to look at his backside.

"You try."

I did, sinking almost immediately.

He growled in his throat when he came back over. "You are determined to test me."

I scowled. "Hey, you're not the one who keeps getting lungfuls of water."

"I'm going to hold you up, under the water, and you are going to move your arms and legs as I tell you." His voice was tight.

"Hold me up?"

"Yes. So that you don't sink for long enough to learn the technique."

"Right."

I moved off the step and felt his strong hands grip me around the waist. He tipped me, so that I was almost facing the bottom of the pool, and I strained to keep my head up.

"Kick your legs, one at a time, with even pace. Stretch out your feet."

I did as he said, but the only part of me I was really aware of was the bit his hands were on.

"Good. Now, your arms." He explained how to move my arms, still holding me firmly in place.

Again, I tried to focus on doing what he said, and mostly failed.

"I'm going to let go now. Try and swim toward the cove entrance."

He let go, and I immediately started to sink. But, as I started to panic-flail, I stopped myself, forcing the movement he had just made me practice into my arms instead. My head raised and I moved a few feet through the water. Excitement rushed me, and I kicked my legs harder.

"Good. Keep your arms and legs in time."

I did, and before I knew it, I was on the other side of the pool.

"Ha!" I turned and straightened. The bottom of the pool was deeper here. I yelped as I went under, and this time really did get a lungful of water.

Strong hands were around my waist again, and I choked down air as he lifted me above the surface.

Carrying me like a spluttering child, he moved us to where it was shallower.

"We will also practice treading water."

23

REYNA

The shock of going under forced me to concentrate on actually swimming instead of Mazrith's body.

I strove to focus on the movements, on each flex and kick, ignoring the heat of his hands on my waist and the occasional brush of powerful legs underwater. I began to feel to the flow and surge of the water, catching the rhythm of kicks and strokes needed to propel myself through the still spring, and once I stopped sinking unexpectedly, started to enjoy it.

Each time I started to feel some speed though, or tried to move my legs wider, my shift stuck to me, tangling between my thighs. I moved to the step.

"I think I would be able to move a lot more easily without this on," I said, my heart pounding as Mazrith gave me a searing look.

"You want to remove your clothing?"

"You can't see me, I'm under the water. It keeps tangling, and I want to go faster."

His jaw set, but he didn't protest again, so I peeled the shift off my body, careful to keep my now bare breasts under the steamy surface. I left my cotton knickers on.

As I pushed off the step, Mazrith slid behind me, guiding my legs and hips into the proper shape for strong kicks. His hands lingered at my thighs, though, and I wasn't sure if they were instructive touches anymore.

With a sudden, decisive movement, he wrapped both hands around my hips and reeled me back against him. I gasped at the press of his arousal against my backside, and he pulled me into him, his chest heaving against my back as he gripped me close. He didn't move though, just held me hard against him.

"*Gildi*," he murmured tightly into my hair. "Tell me to stop."

My heart hammered against my ribs, desire coursing through my entire body as I felt his own heart pound. "No."

The water lapped at my skin. He turned me to face him, hands sliding to grasp my backside to lift me. I wrapped my legs around his waist, buoyed by the water. He pulled me tight against him with a groan, his hardness pressing insistently against the juncture of my thighs, the cotton of my underwear between us. Water rippled over my breasts as Mazrith claimed my mouth in a searing kiss. Our bodies slid and moved together in the warm water, and I grasped at his shoulders for an anchor in the swirling bliss of sensation I was losing myself to.

He groaned into my mouth, every muscle in his torso

grown taut, rocking into each subconscious roll of my hips as waves we were creating lapped and broke around us.

He broke off the kiss and moved, his lips blazing a trail of fire down my throat and across my collarbone. He lifted me higher against his body, raising my breasts from the water. I arched into each caress of his hands and mouth, every nerve alight with sensation. His tongue swirled around one nipple, teasing it to a hardened peak before he sucked and nipped gently. I cried out, tangling my fingers in his hair to keep him there as waves of pleasure radiated outward. He turned his attention to the other, the heat between my thighs building uncontrollably with each touch. By the time his kisses moved down across my belly, I was shaking with sensitivity, ready to do exactly what I told him I wouldn't. Beg for more.

Mazrith moved through the water, me wrapped around his body, until we reached the pool edge. I gasped at the cold of the ice when he turned and set me down. I reluctantly let go of him, staring into his fierce, bright eyes. He ran his fingers along my thighs, then pulled them apart.

The cold of the ice was replaced by searing heat, anticipation lighting my nerves on fire. My breath came hot and fast as he took the material of my underwear between his fingertips and slowly tore it in two, exposing me to him completely. A single fingertip stroked along my slit, drawing forth a rush of wet desire. "I have waited so long to feel you," he hissed. I bit down hard on my lip to stop myself saying anything stupid. Anything that might make him stop. "I wanted to make you beg. I *told* you I would make you beg."

Fuck, I would do more than beg. I was so desperate from

the featherlight touch he was running through my wetness to becoming the pounding pleasure I knew he could deliver, I would do anything.

But he didn't make me say a word. He dropped his head, so fast I cried out in surprise and then pleasure, as his lips closed over the place his fingers had been so delicately teasing.

The pool, the ice, the whole fucking world fell away as my head tipped back and pleasure swallowed me whole. He explored me with lips and tongue and teeth, growling at each movement of my hips urging him on. Two fingers slid inside easily, pumping slowly in and out as he lavished attention on the sensitive nub he'd found so fast.

I clutched at the pool edge beneath me, panting and writhing, as streaks of intensity shot through my body. The pressure built swiftly to an unbearable peak. Mazrith's fingers crooked and twisted, finding a spot within on each plunge inward that made me dizzy with pleasure. His tongue lashed with precision. I tumbled over the edge into frenzy, clamping down on his fingers again and again in waves that seemed endless. He did not stop until I went limp, trembling in the aftermath of pleasure like I had never felt. Mazrith stood back up, expression fierce with desire. I could feel the length of him throbbing heavy and insistent against me. "You taste as sweet as mead," he growled. His hands moved to grasp my hips, and he pressed against my sensitized body, making me gasp.

My breath froze on my lips though, as a flurry of golden runes poured from his bare chest and shoulders, skimming his beautiful face as they floated from him.

There were too many for me to read and he went rigid, his fingers digging into my flesh.

Slowly, he relinquished his grip and backed away from me, the water swallowing his naked body. The runes slowed, then stopped.

My chest heaved as I stared, suddenly aware of my legs wide apart before him. I squeezed them shut and sat up straight.

"Why is that happening?" I rasped out.

"My curse," he growled. "This is what she must have been warning me about."

The haze from the crashing pleasure that had consumed me began to clear. "What? What are you talking about?"

Something that wasn't fear or anger, but that I couldn't place, filled his face. "There are only so many runes," he said quietly.

Confusion, fueled by the need still pounding through me, made me fist my hands. "Please," I said, slowly. "I don't understand."

He bared his teeth, then he pushed his hair back from his face angrily. "When the last gold rune floats from my skin, it is over. And for whatever reason, being close to you makes them fly from my fucking body."

I stared. "You just said *she* warned you."

"My mother. When she told me to find you, she said you were... dangerous."

My stomach twisted. Not just because of what I was apparently doing to Mazrith, but at the word *dangerous*.

There was a darkness in me. I had feared it since the

Starved Ones appeared in my head as a child, and ever since, that fear had only grown. Especially now.

"Dangerous how?" I asked, my voice small.

"She didn't say. Just that I couldn't get close to you."

"Why would I speed up your curse?"

"I do not know."

"Could it be coincidence?" My mind flitted back to the very first day he'd taken me from the Gold Court, on the boat. The gold rune that had floated from his skin when he'd caught me as I fell.

He shook his head. "No. Perhaps any *gold-giver* would accelerate the magic. You are, after all, connected to gold."

I nodded, hope spiking at that possibility. Cold air wafted through the steam, making my exposed, wet chest prickle with gooseflesh. I slipped back into the water, awkward and unsure now, my body still aching with want for him, but the sting of him backing away from me once again making me bite my tongue.

"Reyna... You..." I looked at him as he searched for something to say.

"I...?"

He moved through the water fast enough to make waves lap up to my neck, then took the back of my head in his hands and pressed his lips to mine more tenderly than the ferocity of the move suggested he would. His tongue teased at mine, his lips carrying an apology I didn't think he could make aloud.

And, I hoped, a promise.

A rune floated from his temple as he pulled away, and this time *I* stepped back. "Don't," I said. My voice was throaty and didn't sound like my own. "I don't want to hurt you."

Dangerous.

"We will lift this curse." His voice was even more hoarse than mine. "And when I next lay my hands on you, it will be no dream. It will be the most real, the most consuming, the most obliterating thing you will ever experience. When I take you, it will not just be your body. You will desire for nothing. Never want to leave. You will belong to me."

My knees felt weak in the water. I believed him.

But I already belonged to him.

I glanced down at the rune on my wrist, dark beneath the water, the intensity of the moment blighted by reality.

I'd spent my life running from being owned. Would giving myself to Mazrith, letting him claim my body, really give him my heart and soul too?

Because that was the only way he could truly own me. Love.

A clarity I had never felt before washed over me as I looked into his face. Was that what he had meant in the library? That you could belong to somebody, but still be free?

Could love do that?

His blazing eyes softened. "I have made you fear me. You do not wish to belong to anyone."

For a beat I thought he'd read my mind, but his staff was not in the pool with us. I shook my head slowly. "We are learning to trust each other," I said. "And there is no question of attraction." My heated, aching body and the memory of his hardness against me was undeniable. "But if letting you have my body means I can never leave—"

"I did not say you couldn't leave. Just that you will never want to."

I stared at him, his eyes alight with desire. Passion. There was no arrogance in his words. Just certainty.

"Until the curse is lifted, it doesn't matter," I said, eventually. "I'm not going to risk killing you."

He nodded, eyes still fixed on mine. "We get the mist-staff, we lift the curse. We kill the Queen. And then I will fill the void in your life, *gildi*."

24

REYNA

My mind tumbled with thoughts for the rest of the day and evening. I halfheartedly joined in with conversations around the table during dinner, but my thoughts were stuck on one thing.

Mazrith.

The fae Prince of the Shadow Court.

Every time I looked at him, he was looking at someone or something else, but I was sure I could feel his gaze on me as often as mine was seeking him.

He was quiet too, Frima and Svangrior regularly having to repeat themselves because he had missed what they were saying.

If the curse didn't exist, and I had given myself over to the fae Prince, what would have changed between us?

I didn't love him. I knew that.

I *couldn't* love him.

For so many reasons. All of them played on a loop in my

head, and I wondered why I couldn't just write off what had happened as lust and move on.

I respected Mazrith. I was confident that he had a sort of respect for me. We needed to work together for the sake of the world that we lived in, and powers stronger than us had apparently paved this path for us long ago. These were the facts. The cold, hard, facts.

Feelings were not facts.

When I collapsed into the bed in the cabin, I found myself missing Voror.

"I'm guessing your swim was more than just a swim," said Frima, stripping off her clothes without a shred of modesty.

"It was just a swim," I mumbled into my pillow.

"Uh-huh. Why are you so out of sorts then?"

"I miss my owl."

She raised her eyebrows at me. "You have an owl?"

Figuring that she would no doubt find out about Voror at some point, I nodded. "He can talk to me."

She pursed her lips. "And would you tell *him* the truth about you and Maz if he was here?"

I snorted. "He would likely resume his attempted lesson in human procreation and get twitchy about bodily fluids."

Frima looked at me, eyes flashing. "So, you *were* fucking."

"No. That would... complicate things."

She sighed, pulled a shift over her head, and dragged some furs over her. "I hate to tell you this, but I don't think you two are destined for anything other than complicated."

"You might be right."

. . .

I fell into a fitful sleep, and after my near-death experience in the ice building that morning wasn't surprised to find my dreams plagued by monsters. This time, the Starved Ones were frozen, limbs snapping off and shattering as they sang my name, climbing over each other to get me, piles of mutilated, singing corpses covered in ice everywhere I looked.

I woke early, Frima still sleeping, wrapped Mazrith's cloak around myself and crept out onto the deck. The view out of the cove over the endless frozen sea caught me and I stared out, trying to settle my thoughts. I had another game to complete today. One where I might well drown. Mazrith wouldn't be able to help me if I got into trouble. That much had been proven last time. I tried to fill my head with the memory of the exhilaration of riding Rasa to victory, instead of yesterday's defeat.

"It can be done, Reyna," I said aloud.

I half expected Voror's reply, as he so often did when I was talking to myself. I hadn't been lying when I told Frima I missed him. "If there's any chance you can hear this, Voror, I like it better when you're with me," I whispered.

Life began to stir on the deck a few hours later, Tait and Svangrior rising just after Brynja.

"I guess I won't need my armor today," I told Frima when I went back into my cabin to dress.

"You're not supposed to know the game is swimming," she said.

"Oh. Will I have time to take it off before we start?"

She shrugged. "I have no idea. Is it heavy enough to hinder you?"

"I barely got past flailing around like a child yesterday. Anything would hinder me."

"You should have spent more time practicing and less time fucking then."

I threw my boot at her. She caught it deftly and threw it back. I missed, and it hit me in the shoulder.

Glowering, I tugged it on. "I'm not wearing the armor. Just the finger talons."

"Fine."

Mazrith was as quiet as he had been the day before as we followed our escorts to the whale figurehead boat. Aside from a curt good morning, he hadn't spoken to me. I wondered if he had been up all night, trying to work out why emotions were so infernally confusing.

Maybe it was just lust to him. Possessive lust perhaps, but just lust.

How could a fae prince love a human rune-marked? A weakling with a chip on her shoulder and a defensive streak the size of a palace?

No, it had been arrogance speaking when he'd said I would never want to leave. Or a resignation to the fact that we were bound, and he was stuck with me.

I was back in my own cloak, Mazrith hunched under his and staring out at the plates of ice we were moving between.

He must have felt me looking, because he turned slowly. Rather than look away, I held my gaze. Shadows swirled in his eyes as they met mine, his expression unreadable. Did he regret what happened?

No matter how much confusion it had caused me, I didn't regret a moment. A second, even.

But I hadn't lost precious time to a fatal curse, so I guessed my regret wasn't really comparable.

We approached an iceberg that, unlike the last, had no icy forest blooming across it. It did, however, have the rows of benches that had been present at the last one, along with three huge freestanding mirrors. The other champions were arriving in their boats, and my throat tightened as we climbed onto the ice.

Please, Freya, let this one go better than the last one.

It could hardly go worse.

If Orm hadn't saved your life, it would have been a lot worse, the voice in my head reminded me.

Resolving to do whatever it took to not end up in a position where I would owe that insect anything more, I strode to where the others had been directed.

"You can win this."

Mazrith's voice in my head startled me, and I whipped my head around to look at him as I strode to join the other champions. He had taken a seat in the area designated for shadow-fae, as far from Queen Andask as he was able. His bright eyes fixed on me, his staff held high.

I kept myself from finding the Queen's gaze, though I could feel it trained on me, nodded at him, and turned back.

The Queen of the Ice Court stood and clapped her hands together around her staff. It flashed bright blue, and four large holes appeared in the ice, as though a giant poker had just melted them. Steam rolled from the surface of the water beneath.

Warm water. Relief rushed me. Tait had been right.

"The rules are simple," the Queen called. "Four chests rest on the spring's bottom, anchored in place. Retrieve your chest's contents first, and you win." Her cold eyes glinted. "May victory favor the bold!"

25

REYNA

rm dove beneath the churning water in a splash of bubbles before I could even think about moving. The others followed. Hurriedly, I yanked on my finger talons, held my breath, and jumped in.

My legs flailed instantly as the water covered my head, disorientation taking me. I forced my eyes to stay open, working out where the light was coming from and therefore which way was up.

Looking down as I sank awkwardly through the water, I saw the four chests below, embedded in huge spikes of ice.

Dakkar had already reached his, thick vines sprouting from his staff and burrowing into the ice.

Orm was melting the ice around his with a beam of intense light from his staff as he sank down. Kaldar was the last of the three to reach hers and held her staff to the ice. It vanished instantly.

Orm made a gurgled sound of anger at her, then held up his staff, directing the beam at her instead of his ice spike.

A water-logged shriek hit my ears and Kaldar dropped her staff, throwing her hands up to her eyes. I thought I saw blood streaming between her fingers and a mix of concern and fear rolled through me, followed by a very physical jolt in my feet.

I had reached the bottom.

My lungs were starting to feel tight, and I used the talons on my fingers to claw at the ice, relieved they seemed to work well at the task. I felt a surge of excitement that I was getting through the ice defense so quickly. Dakkar flew upward, an iron sphere in his arms.

Horseshit. He was going to win.

At least it wasn't Orm.

I threw a glance at the gold-fae, and opened my mouth in surprise, water rushing in.

Kaldar had retrieved her staff and now Orm himself was encased in a spike of ice, just as his chest still was. Fury was etched into his face under the glassy surface, and Kaldar stared fixedly at him, scarlet tears running down her grey cheeks.

A burn in my lungs forced my attention back to my chest. I wedged two talons into the gap between the chest bottom and lid and pried it open.

It wasn't just the sense of urgency driven by a need for air that made me snatch the sphere out of the chest. It was the knowledge that I might actually *not lose*.

Kicking my legs, I was alarmed to find the weight of the sphere made my movement harder, and I barely rose a foot off the spring-bottom. It also drew Kaldar's attention to me. It looked like Orm had fallen unconscious in the spike now, and I briefly wondered if he might die in there.

Another burning feeling seared through my chest, and my concern shifted back to myself.

I had to get to the surface. Preferably before Kaldar turned me into an iceblock, or my body betrayed me and tried to take a breath.

I kicked my legs hard and used my free arm to propel me upward, as Mazrith had shown me. Survival instinct seemed to lend strength to my legs, and I moved up through the water, the hole above me both alarmingly far and tantalizingly close.

"You are close. Harder," Mazrith's voice sounded in my head.

Harder.

I thrashed my legs, the pain in my chest now constant and small bubbles escaping me as my breath let out involuntarily.

Harder.

I burst through the surface just as my body relented, gasping in air. There was a surprised chatter of voices, and a couple of half-hearted claps as I kicked at the water, trying to keep myself up. My legs were tired now, though, the sphere heavy, and I dipped back under, spluttering.

Panic propelled me to the edge of the hole, and I grabbed it as I dropped the sphere onto the ice, pulling myself up and out, choking down welcome cool air. The chatter had turned to laughs.

I didn't care though.

Dakkar grinned at me from where he was sitting on the edge of his own hole, holding his sphere. His wet hair, plastered to his head, looked like seaweed.

Kaldar popped up out of her hole as I hauled myself into a sitting position. She held her sphere high, and the crowd roared a cheer. Two gold-fae rushed forward, speaking fast at the Ice King and Queen. I couldn't hear what they were saying, but I could guess.

Could Orm actually die down there?

The King sighed, then looked over at Kaldar. He must have spoken to her telepathically, because her face turned sour, then reluctant, and she dove back into her hole. I stood, the loss of the warm water and the frigid air blowing over my wet clothes making me shiver. I grabbed my cloak and wrapped it around myself as Kaldar emerged from the hole, Orm's unconscious form over one arm.

Dakkar strode over to me on his way to the earth-fae spectators. "I'd say that's a more satisfying end to a game," he said quietly.

"I couldn't agree more." I grinned.

"Look at Queen Andask." His voice was barely more than a murmur.

Her eyes were locked on Orm's unconscious form, now dumped on the ice. The gold-fae had rushed to him, administering some sort of vial to his blue lips. "Does that look like concern to you?"

"Perhaps," I answered, just as quietly. She was certainly more interested in Orm than in me. But *everyone* was watching to see if the arrogant gold-fae Lord would come round.

"I think there is something to their relationship. And that may give them an advantage."

"How?"

"We must not discuss it here. But if allegiances are being formed elsewhere, perhaps it would not be so bad for us to know a little more about each other?"

His words were not sleazy or untoward. They made sense. And Dakkar had tried to help the trick voice in the Shadow Court race. As far as I was concerned, that proved he had a decent heart.

I nodded. "What did you have in mind?"

"I think we will be celebrating my win with a game of kubb. You, your betrothed, and his warriors, would be welcome to join us."

"I'll tell Mazrith."

The earth-fae gave me a knowing kind of look, then strode off with the swagger of one victorious.

I couldn't put the same amount of pride into my walk, but I did keep my chin high as I made my way back to Maz, Frima and Svangrior. Not only had I not drowned, but I had come second.

"Not so fast," rang out the Ice Queen's voice. I paused, looking at her, then at Orm. He was sitting now, apparently conscious. *Curse it.*

"Those of you who managed to retrieve your spheres, please take them with you. If you can open them, the bounty inside is yours." Even from this distance I could see a gleam in her eye.

Was the sphere a trap, or a reward?

Dakkar and I both turned to go back for our spheres.

Kaldar had already taken hers with her. Could she have had prior knowledge? Or was it a tactic to make us think they were safe — they wouldn't attack their own champion, surely?

I peered at the iron as I picked it up off the ice, spying runes I didn't recognize. Trap or not, I had a feeling Tait would delight in it.

"You did well," said Mazrith, when I finally returned to the spectators.

My teeth were chattering a little, but I was nowhere near as cold as the day before, the dry cloak making all the difference. "The swimming lesson helped," I said.

Frima snorted, then turned it into a cough.

"Do you think this is safe to open?" I lifted the sphere, changing the subject.

"Probably not. But I doubt Thor's own hammer would stop Tait from trying."

"That's what I thought. It'll give him something to do while we are out."

Mazrith raised an eyebrow, and Frima leaned in. "Where are we going?" she asked.

"We got an invitation I don't think we should refuse."

26

REYNA

Tait was instantly consumed with the iron sphere, as predicted. He didn't recognize the runes on it either and immediately began flipping through books, muttering incoherently. Even when we all sat down to eat the lamb stew Brynja had made us, he kept a book in his lap, his lips forming silent words as he read.

I hoped that if he did manage to get into the iron ball that he wouldn't be hurt, and that it was indeed a reward.

"Is it likely that the Ice Court would give out gifts?" I asked, swiping bread over the bottom of my bowl to get the last of the delicious gravy.

"I do not know how well-versed King and Queen Verglas are on the etiquette of visiting fae," Mazrith said. He seemed to have cheered a little since the game.

"Did the etiquette used to be to give gifts?" I waved my hand around the cove. "These guest glaciers are pretty amazing, given that they haven't had guests for a long time."

"Maybe they have had guests." We all looked at Tait as he spoke, and he pushed his glasses up his nose and shrugged. "The Shadow Court wouldn't know if the others visited here."

He had a point. Frima looked at me. "Did the Gold Court fae ever visit here?"

I shook my head. "I wasn't party to royal secrets, but as long as I lived in the palace, I never heard of any such thing."

Mazrith spoke. "Gifts would have been given to keep Court allegiances strong," he said, answering my original question.

"So if the Ice Court are trying to do the right thing, unlike your crazy stepmother, that could be safe?" I pointed at the sphere next to Tait's barely touched bowl.

"Yes."

"I won't open it without deciphering the runes," the *shadow-spinner* said. "There's no need to worry."

"I doubt the runes will say danger - this is a trap," Svangrior grunted.

"They will tell me enough, I am sure," Tait answered, then looked back at his book.

"Ho!" A voice called from the ice. Mazrith, Frima, and I stood up to look over the edge of the railings. An earth-fae waved at us, flanked by the same two ice-fae guards who had taken us to the hot spring.

I held a hand up. "Hi."

"Lord Dakkar says he wishes you to join us in kubb. I'm here to take you to the game." He was young, his skin darker than Dakkar's, and his bright green eyes danced with something mischievous.

"We'll be right down."

"I don't trust him," Svangrior growled quietly as he strapped his axe to the side of his body not holding his staff.

"You shock me," Frima said sarcastically.

"Do you?" he barked at her.

"No, but I don't need to trust him." She glanced at me. "Do you trust Dakkar?"

"I think he wants to make sure Orm and Queen Andask don't hurt him or his own, and he is working on the enemy-of-my-enemy-is-my-friend philosophy," I said.

"That's not a yes or a no."

I shrugged. "Because I don't know. But he's not going to hurt us tonight. I'm sure of that."

Mazrith moved beside me, and I turned to him. "Take your talons. In case."

I nodded. I had changed into dry clothes, but stuck with trousers, shirt, and leather wrap, instead of a dress. I had a feeling Dakkar would not care if I dressed as a worker rather than a noble fae-female. I pulled my cloak open enough to show Mazrith my distinctly non-magical staff at my hip, and then pushed my hand into the pocket of my trousers, pulling out a few razor sharp talons. "I may like Dakkar, but I'm not stupid."

His eyes flashed. "I never thought you were."

"So, humans and fae are allowed to marry in your Court, huh?" The young earth fae was looking sideways between me and Mazrith as we followed our ice-fae escorts. His hair was a brighter green than Dakkar's and he was more muscular, less lithe.

"Erm—" I started, but Mazrith cut me off.

"What is your name?"

"Henrik."

"And what are you to Lord Dakkar?"

He shrugged. "A friend."

"Are you a Lord?"

He pulled a face at me that reminded me of Frima, one of playful derision. "Fates, no."

"Why would you not wish to be a Lord?" I asked.

"Far too much talk. Not enough doing." He threw a glance at Frima, something I was sure was flirtation in his eyes.

"Does Dakkar have any family with him here?" Mazrith asked.

Henrik's face turned wary. "Why do you ask?"

"I am curious."

"Do you have family here? Other than Queen Andask?"

"She is not my family." So, it seemed he wasn't going to keep up any charade of being aligned with the Queen to the earth-fae. "And no."

We emerged on the other side of the tunnel, and I raised my eyebrows in surprise.

On the iceberg directly in front of us was a circle of braziers, and the game had been set up in the center. Around each brazier was a layering of furs, and earth-fae were sitting on them, talking and drinking, or watching the game. There were about fifteen fae in total, Dakkar and a female fae standing opposite each other and launching short pieces of wood at their opponent's line of larger, stouter pieces, ten feet away. The short stick hit a post and knocked it over and the woman roared in victory, running across the playing area and punching Dakkar on the arm.

"That," Henrik said, pointing at her, "Is Dak's wife. And she plays a fierce game of kubb. Do you play?"

Everyone except Svangrior nodded, including me. Much like swimming, I had tried to play with the palace kids, but hadn't been welcome, so I had learned on my own. It was a dull game to play by yourself though.

I listened as Frima explained to Svangrior that the idea was to knock over all of the posts on your opponent's side, called kubbs, with your short batons.

"So, say team Thor knocks down three of team Odin's kubbs," she said, and Svangrior nodded. "Then team Odin has to throw his three that fell into team Thor's side of the playing field, then knock those over before they can start knocking over team Thor's actual kubbs."

"What happens when they all get knocked down?"

"Then they have to knock down the central post, called the king, in the middle of the playing field."

"Sounds simple enough," he grunted.

"There are a few more rules than that, but that is the gist," said Henrik. "Come. Dak! Your... *guests* are here!"

Dakkar turned from the game, moving to meet us as we stopped by the warmth of a brazier, and the two ice-fae walked away, back to the edge of the iceberg. Dakkar's wife came with him, and I looked at her with interest. She wasn't wearing a dress. She was wearing clothes similar to mine under her mossy green cloak. Braids filled her dark green hair and her eyes shone with intelligence.

"I'm glad you came," Dakkar said, greeting us. "And just in time to rescue me from being thrashed by my wife. Khadra, This is Prince Mazrith and his betrothed, Reyna..."

"Thorvald," I finished for him. "And this is Frima and Svangrior."

She nodded. "I'm Khadra." She gestured at the kubbs. "Do you play?"

"Yes," Mazrith said immediately.

She smiled. "Then take your time having a drink and meeting our people, and find me when you are ready."

She sauntered away, and Dakkar spoke. "I have no evidence that Orm and Queen Andask are working together," he said, his voice low enough that the fae sitting on the floor nearby could not hear him. "But my instincts tell me that there is more to this *Leikmot* than we know, and that the Gold Court do not seem concerned enough."

"We agree," Mazrith said.

"Do you have any proof?"

"No. The Queen arranged these games as a 'surprise' for my birthday, so I was not involved with any of it."

"It was remarkably easy for you to leave the Gold Court with three captives though," I said, the thought dawning on me as I said it.

Mazrith frowned at me. "You think Orm *let* me take you? His apparent intent on revenge suggests otherwise."

"Good point."

Dakkar shrugged. "My intention in inviting you to our celebration was less to share information, and more to form an allegiance." As much intelligence as had seemed to shine in his wife's eyes danced in Dakkar's. Instinct told me not to blindly trust this fae.

Did he know more was at stake in the Shadow Court than winning a games festival? He must. The discord between Prince and Queen of the same royal family made it clear that no good was coming the way of the shadow-fae.

But aside from winning the *Leikmot*, what ulterior motive could he have?

"We are pleased to be here," Mazrith said a little stiffly, and I knew he was assessing the fae Lord too.

Dakkar gave us both an easy smile. He spread his arms, and called a fae over. "Henrik, get these folk some drinks, would you?" He looked back to us. "Enjoy. Talk to our people. See that we are who you wish us to be."

"And prove to them we are who *you* wish *us* to be?" Mazrith said quietly.

Dakkar's smile widened. "I trust them."

Translation: I don't trust you.

This was an exercise in working each other out, I realized. He strode away, back to the game with his wife. They teamed up with two other fae, staying on opposite sides.

The fae he had called over passed me a cup made from smooth, polished wood. "Thank you. What is it?"

"Nettle wine," he grinned. He must only have been a teenager.

"Do you not have human thralls to hand out drinks here?" asked Frima.

He shook his head. "No. Not since the sickness. But I don't mind. I like helping. Is it true you make staff for those greedy gold-fae?" He stared at me with huge green eyes.

"Sickness?" Mazrith said, before I could respond. "What sickness?"

A female hustled over, slight panic in her eyes, as she laid her hand firmly on the boy's shoulder. He was as tall as she was, but she pulled him back, away from us. "A few human clans have been visited by an unwelcome sickness recently, but it's nothing." She gave the boy a look and he blinked at her, then back at me.

"Do you make staffs for the gold-fae?" he repeated.

"Not anymore," I said, realizing the truth of the words as I said them. Would I ever work with gold again? The thought caused a pang of panic, a lost feeling, to close around me. I concentrated on the boy. "Do you have any *wood-workers* here? I would love to speak with a rune-marked for the earth-fae."

The female looked at me suspiciously. "No."

"Oh. What happens if Dakkar's staff is damaged in the games?"

The suspicion in her eyes deepened a moment, then she looked flustered. "I mean, yes. Of course we do. So, there's no point in targeting Dak's staff," she said quickly.

"I'm not looking for ways to sabotage him," I said gently. "We're here to try to become allies."

"Hm. Well, why don't I introduce you to some more folk." She seemed keen not to be the only one talking to us, and a lot of the other fae were throwing curious glances our way.

"Good," said Mazrith.

She walked us around all the braziers, introducing us to everyone as we went. I knew I had no chance of remembering all the names. Nobody was sneering or cold, but all had a reservation to their manner. All except Henrik, who regularly joined whichever group we were part of, and almost always seemed to end up standing or sitting next to Frima.

Eventually, a huge roar went up from the kubb area, followed by cheering. Dakkar strode over to us, shaking his head.

"I almost had her," he said. "I think it's your turn to try."

"How many to a team?"

"Four will work fine. Shadow Court versus Earth Court?"

"Is that a good idea?" I asked quietly. The folk of *Yggdrasil* were raised to detest losing. And someone would lose.

"I think we can manage a friendly game. After all, folk's true natures are tested in games of valor and skill. And at least I get to be on my wife's side this time." He grinned.

Mazrith nodded. "Absolutely. And perhaps a forfeit, for the loser?"

Dakkar's brows flew up. "You have a team member who has never played before, and I have a tried and tested champion. And yet you are so sure of your upcoming victory?"

"My team will win," said Mazrith.

"What forfeit do you suggest?"

"The team who loses jumps in the sea. Naked," called Henrik.

The fae all laughed, and Dakkar and Mazrith's gazes met. "Let's do it," Dakkar said.

I groaned. "I won't survive that water," I muttered.

"Then we'd better win," answered Frima.

"Ahem." An ice-fae guard coughed, and we all spun to her, surprised by her presence. "None of you will survive that water. It is infested with creatures that would kill you before your head even dipped under the surface."

"Oh."

She swallowed, looked down, then found Dakkar's green eyes again. "But, if you are looking for a good forfeit, I could create a decent snow drift for you. It won't be deadly, but it'll be cursedly cold."

Dakkar gave her a huge smile. "Do you two want to play with us?"

She paused. "There are only two of us. Not enough for a team."

"One of you can join us, and the other the earth-fae," Mazrith said.

"I will play with the Shadow Court," she said immediately, before turning and calling over the other guard. They spoke quickly, and he looked shy as he joined us. Dakkar clapped him on the shoulder.

"What are your names?"

"I am Maya, and this is Erik."

"The forfeit may not mean much to you," Dakkar said, eyeing their mostly naked bodies, "but I sure as Odin don't want my dick covered in snow. Let's win this."

27

REYNA

"Huh. Who knew Svangrior was so well endowed?"

"Frima!" I punched her on the arm, trying to avert my eyes from the stark naked warrior throwing himself into the snowdrift Maya had just made.

We had lost the kubb game pretty resoundingly, thanks to Dakkar's wife being every bit as good as he said she was.

Svangrior, though not responsible for our loss, had surprised everyone by volunteering to take the forfeit for the whole team.

"I feel bad he's doing it alone," Frima said. "He hit more kubbs than I did."

"Feel free to join him," I muttered. "I'm sure-as-Odin not going to."

She shrugged, then began to strip out of her clothes. "Honor is honor," she said.

I gaped at her and pointed as Svangrior extracted

himself from the snow, shivering and hopping from foot to foot as the earth-fae cheered and whooped. "It's freezing."

"I'll find a way to warm up," she said, straightening. She gave me a wink, roared a battle cry, then sprinted at the snow drift.

"Your warriors are mad," I said, shaking my head.

"They are fierce and valiant," Mazrith answered, pride in his voice. And a hint of amusement, I was sure. "I have had an idea."

Henrik met Frima as she tumbled out of the snow, holding a pile of furs. I could swear that whatever he was saying to her was making her cheeks tinge with pink.

"An idea, huh?"

"Yes. I think we should try to get the ice-fae female to drink more wine than she should."

I frowned. "You want to get her drunk?"

"Yes. So she doesn't know I am in her mind."

My mouth fell open. "No! You can't do that to her. She trusts us. She played on our team."

His face was tense. "And under normal circumstances I would honor, and build upon, that trust. But she will know what tomorrow's game is."

"No. It doesn't feel right," I hissed, shaking my head. "And if you are caught, then you'll lose the trust of every-body here."

"Reyna, you surviving is more important than all of this," he said through gritted teeth.

I screwed my face up in annoyance. "Let me talk to her. She might tell me willingly."

"You will rouse suspicion."

"No, I won't."

He gave me a look, and I sighed. "You said you thought she didn't disapprove of our betrothal?"

He nodded. "Correct. And the fact that she joined us tonight reinforces that."

"Then let me see if I can use that to get a conversation going. If it doesn't work, then we'll reconsider your suggestion."

He stared at me, indecision in his eyes. "Fine," he said eventually.

Before he could change his mind, I turned away and headed toward Maya.

"You played well." I smiled when I reached her. My eyes were drawn to her staff immediately, and she followed my gaze.

She lifted it slightly toward me. "You make these for the gold-fae?"

I nodded. "Yours look very different."

"That is not surprising. As fae, we are very different," she said. She glanced over my shoulder, I guessed at Mazrith. I looked too. He was standing on his own watching some of the younger fae play kubb, while the older fae all sat on their blankets drinking and talking.

"He seems different, even from his own kind," she said.

"You know, I think he is."

She looked intently at me a moment. "Do his people accept you?"

"No, not really. I was put into these games by the Shadow Court to prove myself. Not by Mazrith." I didn't elaborate on the fact that it was part of the Queen's plan to prove Mazrith himself incapable of ruling.

Maya looked a little disappointed. "You can't win the *Leikmot*," she said.

I bristled. "You don't know that."

The look she gave me wasn't one of pity, more of resigned futility. "You are human."

Maybe not. The thought popped into my head, and I squashed it.

"I'm getting the impression you think humans and fae should be allowed to... spend more time together?"

She straightened, eyes narrowing. "Of course not. It is inappropriate."

She was lying. I shrugged and pointed at her staff instead. "The work in these is incredible."

Her defensiveness eased away as she smiled at her staff. "It is. The rune-marked are very talented."

Hearing her speak of the rune-marked with respect was something I had never heard in the Gold Court, and I warmed to her more. "How many different gems do they use?"

She eyed me suspiciously. "Why do you wish to know so much about my staff?"

"I'm rune-marked," I said, pointing at my covered wrist. "It's in my blood to be fascinated by staffs, I can't help asking."

"Hm. You would tell me about your gold staffs?"

"Sure. What would you like to know?"

She pursed her lips. "How long do they take you to make?"

"It depends, but three to six weeks usually."

She tilted her head. "Ours are made in half that time."

"Really? Do you have to forge the gems yourself? We must shape the gold from lumps usually."

"Ah, that is surely why it is quicker. Our gems come from the mines in their god-bidden forms."

"So many different gems too," I said, staring at the staff top. "This one, is it a diamond?"

"Yes. And there are two more here, and a ruby from the *grafa* mine here." Pride laced her words.

"All from mines in your own Court?"

"Of course. The diamond mine is the largest, but you can only get the gems at precise times of day, when the light hits the deposits correctly."

"Do you have human thralls working in the mines?"

"No. Only fae may be trusted inside *Jokull*."

"*Jokull?* Is it a sacred place?"

She looked over her shoulder and pointed. "It is the glacier the palace resides on. Although," she looked around herself and lowered her voice. "I do believe tomorrow's game will be held there. Some sort of race, and you and Lord Dakkar will start at a disadvantage due to your failure in the first game."

"Really? What kind of race?"

"I do not know any more. Please, do not tell anyone I told you anything. But, I would see you do well in these games. Or at the least, survive them."

"I appreciate that," I said, meaning it whole-heartedly.

COURT OF MONSTERS AND MALICE

"Did you hear all of that?" I asked Mazrith when we were alone.

"Yes."

"I told you I could get information without making her suspicious."

He gave me a look that said he didn't agree.

"What? She didn't get suspicious! Much."

"She did not give you much information."

"She gave me plenty. Races are good," I said.

"I doubt it will be on horseback. More likely sleds or boards."

"Boards?"

"That fix to your boots and keep you from sinking into the snow."

I screwed my face up, not liking the sound of that at all. "They do that here?"

He nodded, but Svangrior headed toward us, a slight stumble to his gait, and we stopped talking. "I think it is time I retired to my bed, Maz," he said. His voice was a little slurred. He had been sitting with three of Dakkar's warriors, playing some sort of drinking game, and it appeared that the wine may have gotten the better of him.

"I will retire too," I said. The more sleep I had before a game, the better.

Frima opted to stay with the earth-fae and Maya escorted the rest of us back to our boat. "Why is she staying with them?" grumbled Svangrior as we sailed over the quiet waves toward our glacier.

"I think it has to do with Henrik," I said.

Svangrior gave me a sharp look, at odds with his not-so-sharp movements. "Henrik?"

"Yes."

He snorted, then glared at the water.

When we reached the ship Brynja had gone to her bed, but Tait was still up, the sphere in front of him on the table and his face buried in a book. He gave us an absent wave as we boarded.

"Get some sleep and be prepared for whatever comes your way." Mazrith said to me when we were standing outside our cabins. "You have won one race. You can win another."

At the thought of the last race something occurred to me. "Maz," I said as he started to turn. He stopped instantly, eyes fixing on mine. "I've just realized something." My voice was a whisper, but I knew only Tait could hear us. "I haven't had a vision since being in the Ice Court."

"Do you think that means anything?" he asked, frowning.

"I have no idea. That if I have magic it only works in the Shadow Court? Or that someone or something in the Shadow Court is causing the magic?"

"Or it only works when your owl is with you."

My eyebrows flew up. I hadn't made that connection. "You think Voror could be doing it?" I shook my head. "If he is, I don't believe he knows he is."

"I know you won't tell me where he has come from, but it is strong magic that can make wild animals speak."

"I don't know that I would call him wild."

Mazrith gave me a look. "You know what I mean."

COURT OF MONSTERS AND MALICE

"I'll ask him. When we get back to *Yggdrasil*."

"You may find that the game tomorrow triggers them," Mazrith said.

To my surprise, I found myself hoping they would. They wouldn't have saved my life in the first game, nor would they have allowed me to win the second. But during the Shadow Court games they had helped immensely, and I could do with all the help I could get.

28

MAZRITH

For the second night running, sleep eluded me.

How was I supposed to find rest when she was in the cabin next to me?

I had gone too far already and paid the price. The memory of the golden runes rushing from my skin made me want to tear the tiny room apart.

Svangrior snored beside me, and I forced my fists to relax.

Once the runes ran out, I could not help her. I could not take that risk. Could not leave her to face the *Leikmot*, my stepmother, and the rest of our quest alone.

I burned for her though, and now I knew for sure that she wanted me as much as I wanted her.

But she didn't feel for me in the same way. How could she? I was years ahead of her.

Guilt washed through me. I had made her tell me her

darkest secrets. Yet, there were still so much I was keeping from her.

Fear kept my lips sealed. Fear that she would not forgive me, and our quest would be abandoned. That could not happen, as much for her own sake as mine.

I was sure now that seeking the mist-staff was her destiny as much as it was my own.

She was not human. And someone out there knew who she was. *What* she was. Would they seek to take advantage of her when she found what we were looking for?

I needed that staff. I needed it for more than vanquishing my stepmother and keeping my Court safe.

I needed it to keep her safe.

I rose early, sitting at the table and staring out at the view I had watched Reyna stare out at the previous morning. The solitude made no dent in my turmoil.

When Reyna emerged from her cabin a few hours later, I was forced to tamp down a burning anger that it had been Frima who had helped her into her feather-plate armor, rather than me.

Her hair was tied up, but her new braid stood out in the silky mass of copper. Her fingers were tipped with the talons, and she wiggled them at me as she came over to the table. "I don't know if I can drink coffee with these on."

"Fuck the coffee. Go straight for the mead," Frima said, doing exactly that. She had returned to the boat not long after I had risen, though I had made sure she didn't see me.

Reyna looked at her a moment, then shrugged. "It's restorative, and I might die in a few hours. Why not?"

Frima tugged a bottle of mead from one of the storage chests and poured them both a glass. Reyna's words rolled through my head. *I might die in a few hours.*

"Maz? Want some?"

Echoing Reyna, I nodded. "Why not."

The three of us clinked our glasses.

"To Reyna's imminent victory," Frima grinned at her.

Reyna smiled back, without the confidence of the fae warrior making the toast.

"You have won one race already," I said, my throat constricting as her eyes locked on mine. Fear, determination, and maybe hope, shone in their green depths.

Her lips pressed together tightly. "Orm will have a point to prove this time."

"Kaldar was the one who knocked him unconscious," Frima snorted. "Let those two sort it out."

She was still worried about the lack of visions, I realized, as I watched her sip her mead. They had helped her win the last race, and so far here, she had received no such help.

Fates, I wished I had some idea what she was, and how to help her.

But all I knew was that she was special. Destined.

Mine.

The word flew into my head, and I stood, turning away from the table, and her.

Frima swore, my movement startling her into spilling her drink. I swept to the railings and glared out.

"Mazrith?" Reyna's soft voice saying my name made every muscle in my body clench.

"It is time to go." I said, schooling my face, and turning back. "If you can't win, second will keep you in with a chance. Just don't die."

29

REYNA

When we reached the end of the tunnel, the whale figurehead boat was waiting with Maya and Erik. Nervous silence settled over everyone as we floated between the icebergs, and I noticed that the route carefully took us away from the side of the glacier that housed the palace, skirting instead to the other side of the colossal edifice. I could understand the ice-fae royals for being so secretive, after what Queen Andask had done, but I wished I had seen the palace.

"It looks like a bright blue mountain," I murmured, staring at the glacier. "I wonder if the palace is as big as the one in the Gold Court."

"My mother always wished to see the palaces in every Court," Mazrith said quietly. I looked at him, anger flashing in his eyes before it faded and he focused on me. "I doubt many surviving fae have."

"She wanted the fae to work together?"

"Yes. To trade knowledge as well as goods. Each of the Courts are so different. She believed the power that could come of combining materials and magic would be enormous." I saw Maya glance back at us as he spoke.

"I bet she and Tait got on well."

"Yes."

We rounded the base of the mountainous glacier and reached an area where the incline was much gentler. An icy shore jutted out into the sea, with the now familiar setup of spectator benches and large mirrors that showed the crowd what was out of their line of sight. Beyond the shore that was fast filling with chattering fae was a forest that climbed gradually up the side of the glacier before the steepness resumed, the trees thick with snow that sparkled bright enough in the light to make me squint.

"Infernal fucking light," growled Svangrior as we climbed out of the boat. I was inclined to agree with him.

Kaldar and Orm had yet to arrive, but Dakkar was standing near the two thrones occupied by King and Queen Verglas.

"Wish me luck," I muttered.

"You do not need it."

Queen Andask swept past us, toward the seats where the shadow-fae were sitting. "Ah, Mazrith, dear. I was going to save the seat next to mine for you," she beamed at him, before looking at me. "The last game was close," she said, her eyes gleaming. "Such fine entertainment, this *Leikmot.*"

"I'm sure. Is Lord Orm feeling better now?" I watched her face for a reaction, rewarded with a minute flicker of her overly sweet smile.

"How would I know?"

Before anyone could answer, Lord Orm's boat pulled up alongside the shore, folk pointing and chattering louder. He climbed out easily, apparently fully recovered, and strode toward the other champions. A sigh of disappointment left my lips as a snarl escaped Mazrith's.

The Queen smirked at him, then moved to her seat.

"Win, Reyna," Mazrith hissed through his teeth, before following her.

"I'll try." I moved to stand with the others, just as King Verglas clapped his hands and everyone's attention snapped in his direction.

"Welcome to the last game in our Court," he called. "This is a race. There are scarves attached to many of the trees in the forest. The first to claim all in their color will win. Orm is gold, Dakkar is green, Kaldar is blue, and Reyna is black. Lord Orm and Lady Kaldar will start with one flag each as per the advantage from the last game."

Nerves made my stomach tight. There was no heavy lifting or magic needed, unless the flags were impossible to reach. I glanced at the trees I could see through the uneven snowy terrain. None looked too tall.

Queen Verglas stood up next to her husband and clapped her hands. Four sleds came gliding out of the forest, each pulled by three huge, shaggy white dogs. One by the one, the dogs stopped their sleds in front of each of the champions. They were all nearly as large as I was, their yellow eyes regarding me as I tried to exude a confidence I didn't really feel.

"Hi," I whispered. Hesitantly, I climbed onto the wooden sled, taking the reins.

A gong sounded, and the other three sleds took off with a roar from each fae.

My sled did not move. I snapped the reins and called to the dogs over the laughter of the spectators.

"Please move," I willed the animals. "There's food for you at the end of this." I didn't know if that was true, but mercifully, they began to pull my sled towards the trees.

The other three sleds had gone right on entering the forest, but I spotted movement in a thick cluster of trees right on the forest edge, the snow mostly kept off the lower branches.

A group of flags tied to a high branch. I pulled hard on the reins, to stop the dogs.

"Please, please, wait here for me," I begged them, leaping off the sled. The lead dog eyed me, and I gave her a broad smile. "Steaks. I'll make sure they find you steaks."

More laughter rippled through the fae spectators as I wrapped myself around the slim tree trunk and began to climb. I couldn't use magic to get the flag down, so this would have to do.

Mazrith's voice growled into my mind as I worked on the knot securing the flag. "Every single *veslingr* here who mocks you will live out their worst fucking nightmares when I get them alone."

"Thanks, Maz," I whispered, as I snatched the black flag from the branch, and shimmied back down the tree. Leaping back onto the sled, I pulled on the reins and the dogs took off immediately. One down, Freya-only-knew how many more to go.

The icy forest flashed by as I urged the dogs onward, racing over frozen streams and around massive trees, some free and shaking with the speed of my passing sled, and others completely entombed in ice. Orm, Dakkar and Kaldar must be ahead of me after my slow start, and they didn't have to stop to climb infernal trees to get their flags. I gritted my teeth, determined to catch up.

My dogs picked up speed, navigating icy ramps and hairpin turns through the trees until we shot out of the forest onto a frozen lake. I could see the trees at the other end of the expanse of glittering ice, but barricades and obstacles had been set up like a maze, clearly to make it hard for us to get there. I took a deep breath and snapped the reins.

We slid around sharp corners, raced over bumps that launched us briefly into the air, and zoomed down icy dips that threatened to overturn the sled. But the dogs were well-trained, responding to my every command, and I suspected they had done this before. And that the promise of steak was working. We were halfway across the lake when I spotted Orm up ahead, stopped near a group of flags atop a sharp spike of ice.

He turned with a snarl as I approached, raising his staff. A wall of light erupted from the end, and I forced my eyes closed, remembering Kaldar's bleeding eyes. I yanked the reins with all my might, just avoiding collision with the spike, but my sled tipped precariously, and I tumbled onto the ice. Pain shot through my left ankle. I scrambled to my feet, ignoring the pain, and launched myself at the spike, swiping for the black flag.

Orm lashed out with his staff, catching me on the shoulder. My armor ensured I felt no pain, but the force was enough to shove me backwards. He laughed, snatched his own flag, then roared at his dogs. They sped away as I hurled insults at his retreating back.

Hands shaking, it took me a few attempts to get high enough up the slippery spike to get my own flag.

Where in Odin's names were the visions? If I'd known he had been about to blind me, I could have halted earlier.

I righted my sled with an effort, the dogs pawing at the ice, then climbed back on. Perhaps bored of waiting, the dogs exploded into motion. I grabbed the reins, struggling to stay on the sled while keeping up our speed, my heart racing.

We glided over a series of ramps, sailing high into the air before landing jarringly back on the ice. The impacts rattled my sore ankle, but we didn't slow down.

Up ahead, the track curved between massive spikes of ice, leaving little room to maneuver. I took a deep breath and loosened the reins to let the dogs do what they did best, but the ice beneath my runners suddenly lurched and cracked, throwing me violently to the side. I tumbled onto the unforgiving surface a second time, my sled overturning and skidding out of reach.

Dazed, I pushed myself up, but my leg refused to

support my weight - my ankle had been reinjured in the harsh fall. An ominous creaking filled the air and the ground shuddered under my hands and knees. To my horror, a chasm was opening between the dogs and I, widening rapidly. Through the mass of tangled leads, I could see the dogs straining in their harnesses, but they were still attached to the heavy upturned sled and the runners that usually allowed it to move were facing the sky, the splintered wood spiking into the ice instead, anchoring it. I began dragging myself toward them, grimacing against the pain. They snarled and snapped in panic as the ice under their feet split and tilted, the sled sliding toward the abyss. I scrambled to the very edge of the fissure and stretched out my arm, struggling to reach the lead dog's harness.

With a hiss of relief, I closed my fingers around the clasp, pulling it open. As the sled tipped into the yawning crack, the biggest dog launched herself forward, the others still tied to her. Sharp claws dug into the ice, giving her grip, and then she was bounding away. I let out my breath as the others scrambled after her, away from the chasm.

The ground lurched beneath me, and my breath caught once more. I was so caught up in their escape that I'd not realized how fragile the ice under my own body was.

I pushed myself backwards on my backside, scooting as fast as I could over the slippery surface. But cracks were breaking off from the main chasm now, fast and furious.

I tried to push to my feet but stumbled again. When my hands went down to catch my weight, they found no ice. Just thin air.

My scream was lost as I tipped into the darkness below.

30

REYNA

Cold.

It was the first thing I was aware of as consciousness slowly filtered back.

I was freezing.

How in the name of Odin was I even alive?

I forced my eyes open.

Snow. All I could see around me was snow. Claustrophobic panic instantly set in.

I was trapped.

I tried to move, but every limb hurt, my own weight too much to bear. The snow above me shifted, clearly not as deep or thick as what was below and around me, and I clawed at it, trying to clear a path with my aching arms.

How had I even survived?

Did it matter, since I was presumably at the bottom of a chasm encased in freezing snow that would kill me within a few hours anyway?

My tired clawing grew more frantic, and I cleared the snow from around my face. Darkness yawned above me, a long crack of bright light at the very top. My already skipping heart stuttered.

"Stay still. I am coming to you."

Mazrith's voice in my mind halted the spiraling panic in its tracks. Hot tears stung at my eyes. Never had I been so relieved to hear anyone's voice.

"Oh, blessed Freya, thank you," I mumbled, my lips chattering.

How would he get down to me? It wouldn't surprise me if half the infernal bones in my body were broken, my limbs were so unresponsive.

Maybe his shadows could lift me out?

A scream of surprise burst from my lips, the sound raw and scratchy, as the snow underneath me suddenly gave way.

As though I were inside a tunnel, I flew downward, and only stopped shrieking when I saw a flicker of black swishing around me.

"Maz?!"

"I am bringing you to me."

A second later I tumbled out of the snow, too dazed and cold to take in anything other than the strong arms that caught me.

Heat rolled from Mazrith's body as he lowered me down, setting me across his lap. In a swift movement he removed my wet cloak and then tugged me back against his chest, tucking me inside his own furs.

"Drink." A hand appeared under the fur, holding a flask.

Praying it was mead, my numb fingers grasped it and I drank greedily. Blessed heat washed through my body.

"Is anything broken?"

"I-I don't know."

I tipped my head back and looked into his face. His expression was hard, but I could see the concern in his eyes. I forced my gaze away and peered out at the rest of the space. "Are we in a cave?"

"Yes. Inside the glacier, under the chasm." I shivered and he pulled me tighter against him, almost closing the cloak over my head. "You must keep your head warm," he said, more gently. "Drink all of the mead."

"I will," I said from against his chest. "What happened?" I was starting to warm up already and sipped more of the drink as he spoke.

"I don't know what caused the crack, but I do not believe it was an accident. When it appeared and I saw you fall, I caused a… *distraction* amongst the spectators and came to find you. I also broke the mirrors."

"So nobody can see us right now?"

"No. I do not believe so."

"Why did you do that?"

His body tensed and I wished I could see his face. "If you were not dead, whoever caused the fall might have come to finish the task if they could see you were still alive."

I paused before asking, "Did you think I was dead?"

"No. Snow is excellent at breaking falls, and your armor is strong. But I knew the cold would kill you if I didn't find you fast enough."

"Are the ice-fae looking for me too?"

"Yes. But they can't find you through your ring. I can."

We lapsed into silence as I drank more mead and felt the life coming back into my limbs. They weren't broken, I realized as I began to tentatively move them. They had just been numb from the cold.

"Do you wish to stand?"

"Yes. I hurt my ankle, so I don't know how well I'll be able to walk."

He placed his hands around my waist, helping me to stand. Warmth spread from his palms, and I resisted the urge to crawl back inside his cloak and press myself against him.

I got my balance, looking around the cave. The tunnel he had burrowed through the snow to get to me was behind me, and three more tunnels led off the area. The walls and ceiling were made of ice, sparkling in the gloom with enough light to see well. About the same amount of light as the Shadow Court had, in fact.

"How is your ankle?"

I took a testing, stumbling step. "Not broken. Twisted, maybe."

"Here."

I turned to him, and he handed me a dry cloak. Frima's cloak, I recognized.

I took it gratefully and wrapped it around my shoulders.

His bright eyes bore into mine and I once again felt the urge to move to him. To thank him for showing up exactly when I needed him. For saving my life. Again.

"We need to leave this place," he rumbled.

"I am strong enough. But we'll have to move slowly."

"It is not far."

I leaned on his arm, limping as we entered the tunnel on the left, trying to work out how to walk with the least pain. The tunnel ascended steeply, pale blue walls sparkling with diamond dust, and when we reached the next cave, I stopped to stare.

Veins of raw diamonds glinted in the icy surface like stars, knotted together in clusters wherever the chisels and picks of miners had carved. Massive carved columns of ice supported a ceiling encrusted with dagger-sharp icicles.

"We're in a diamond mine," I breathed.

"Yes. It was the fastest way to get deep enough to reach you." He glanced at me. "If we are caught by the ice-fae in here, whatever our reasons, I cannot see it ending well. If we were to be accused of theft whilst in the Ice Court by invitation..."

I nodded my understanding and tried to hobble faster alongside him.

We moved through more tunnels and caves, all sloping uphill, until eventually I saw light up ahead. The bottom of the chasm I had plunged into must have been well below sea-level, because when we came out of the tunnel it was into a tiny cove. The whale figurehead boat was bobbing there, an ice-fae female looking around anxiously.

"Maya!"

"Hurry," she said, gesturing her hands fast. "If I am caught, it will be more than my position as guard that I lose."

Mazrith bundled me onto the boat and she propelled it

through the ice passages much faster than we had moved before.

"Maya stopped me running into the forest during the confusion," Mazrith said. "She told me she knew a faster way."

"I am grateful. Thank you."

She gave me a dark look. "Freya knows why I feel compelled to keep helping you," she muttered.

"I have an idea why," I said softly. "You have a human friend that you wish could be more."

She glared, but didn't deny it.

"When I am king of the Shadow Court and have a human bride on the throne beside me, perhaps your royal family will change their views on those unions," Mazrith said, his voice surprisingly gentle. My heart thudded at his words, and I forced out the image they caused. I was no queen, and I had no space in my head to process the idea of being one.

Maya looked at him, her mouth tight, but there was a glint of hope in her eyes. "To admit to even thinking about such unions would cost more than I can give," she said. "But... perhaps. One day things may be different." She lapsed into silence as we powered on, and within a few more moments, the little boat reached a tiny shore, the forest looming beyond.

"Get out here, and walk through the forest to the main shore," Maya said, pulling us to a stop.

We scrambled out of the boat as fast as my ankle would allow.

"You will always be welcome in my Court, when I am

King," Mazrith said. Maya nodded at him, then pushed her boat off, moving fast through the water.

"I told you not to mess with her trust," I whispered as we stepped into the trees.

"And you were right."

I raised a brow, but he didn't look at me, just helped me limp faster.

When we emerged from the forest a few painful minutes later, it was to chaos.

All the large mirrors had been smashed, broken glass littering the shore. Fae were everywhere, many wide-eyed, staffs glowing all different colors as they tried to get into the *karves* lining the shore.

Ice-fae guards stood before the boats, refusing to let anyone leave.

"I must find my warriors. If they have been held responsible for my distraction, they could be in trouble," Mazrith rumbled.

"What did you do?"

A wicked glint gleamed in his eyes as he looked at me. "I called on some of the local wildlife."

I frowned, then realized what he must mean. "Snakes?"

"Sea snakes. There are some incredible specimens in these waters."

"Prince Mazrith!" A voice bellowed over the chaos, and everyone fell silent a moment, looking over at us. "You have found Reyna."

Dakkar strode toward us, then turned to an ice-fae guard with almost white-blue hair and more braids than I could try to count. "She has been found," he said, gesturing at me. "Now may we leave?"

"King and Queen Verglas have been moved to safety, I must confer with them," the ice-fae answered, loud enough for everyone to hear.

He turned away, and his staff glowed.

"Moved to safety? Was the threat the chasm or your snakes?"

"I think the Prince's snakes," said Dakkar, reaching us. "What happened?"

I told him about the chasm opening under me, as his wife, Frima, Svangrior, and Henrik peeled away from the crowd waiting for boats and came over.

Frima moved straight to me, clapping my shoulder. "Thanks for the cloak," I told her.

"You're welcome. You know, somebody is definitely trying to kill you."

"I'm happy to tell you that they've failed so far."

"It can't be that limp-dick gold-fae." Svangrior thrust his arm out at Maz. There were two bright red blisters on his skin under his torn shirt. "Next time you summon snakes, can you tell them we're not the enemies before you fucking disappear?"

A tendril of shadow zoomed from Mazrith's staff and wrapped itself around Svangrior's wound. The warrior grimaced.

"King and Queen Verglas wish to convey their regret that the last game was interrupted by saboteurs," the ice-fae guard boomed. We all turned to him. "As such, they request that this round of the *Leikmot* comes to an end, and our visitors return home. At the point the last game was halted, Lady Kaldar had the most flags, and is therefore declared the winner." There was a smattering of applause and whoops from the ice-fae spectators.

The guards keeping people away from the boats moved, and the fae started to fill the small vessels, apparently just as keen to leave as the Ice Court King and Queen were for them to.

I shivered, still cold and sore. I would not be sorry to leave myself.

"I believe the next round will be hosted in the Earth Court," Dakkar said to Mazrith, then looked at me. "Wait for word from our emissaries. If you can stay alive until then." He flashed me a grin, then strode away with Khadra, who gripped his hand tightly.

"He thinks it is funny that someone is trying to kill you so brazenly?" growled Mazrith at his retreating figure.

"No. I think grinning is just his thing."

"How did the game go?" called Tait cheerfully when we reached our boat.

"Not so good," I said, then squeaked as Maz lifted me bodily and leaped up onto the deck. He set me down at the table.

"Mead, Brynja," he said, and she hurried off with a concerned look at me. "Tait, can you bind Reyna's ankle?"

"Of course." He set his books down and dug gauzy material out of a bag on the planks as I pulled my boot off, wincing. Mazrith moved to the front of the boat and held up his staff. Shadows rushed out, moving to fill the sail.

We left the cove quickly, our boat bumped by sheets of ice on each side, funneled into a passageway behind another much larger boat. I realized with a scowl that the style was incredibly similar to our own. It was the Queen's boat.

Tait wound a fabric around my ankle and it felt better immediately with the support. "Who won the game?" he asked as he worked.

"Kaldar," I sighed. "At least it wasn't Orm." But that was one more win to each of the other champions. I had achieved very little in the Ice Court, past possibly making some new friends. And discovering that having sex with Mazrith might kill him.

I knocked back the rest of my mead. "If nobody minds, I need my bed."

31

REYNA

They let me sleep until we reached the tree. The mead had worked its magic whilst I slept, and I felt much better, if very stiff, when I dressed quickly in my trousers and leathers.

I was looking forward to seeing Voror. I didn't believe there were any threats in such a beautiful place, but it would be reassuring to see that he was okay all the same. And I wanted to ask him about Mazrith's idea that he was causing my visions. I hadn't had a single one in the Ice Court.

And I hadn't won a single game.

My ankle was awkward, but not painful, as I stepped out onto the deck. The huge ice doors set into the trunk of *Yggdrasil* before us were already open, and I raised my eyebrows.

"The Queen has just gone through." Frima handed me a mug of nettle tea.

"Thanks. I take it there's been no trouble on the root-river while I was resting?"

"Trouble? You mean with the Queen?"

No, hordes of Starved Ones looking for me. "Yeah."

"No. It's been quiet."

Mazrith stood at the snake figurehead as we sailed through the doors and into the warm, inviting light of the interior. The Queen's ship was already out of sight. Mazrith's shadows whispered around the sails, and we slowed almost to a stop.

"Voror?" I whispered.

The owl swooped down almost immediately. I beamed at him as he landed on the railings, barely stopping myself from reaching out and petting him. There was no way in Valhalla he would appreciate that.

"How are you?"

"Well. This sanctuary suits me, though there is little to eat."

"No rats inside the sacred tree, huh?" I was aware of everyone staring at me, only hearing my side of the conversation, but I ignored them.

"None. How did you fare in the games?" His huge eyes scanned my hair. Looking for a braid. I felt a twist of shame but swallowed it down.

"I won none, and somebody tried to kill me in two of them."

"Ah."

"Ah, indeed. How did you"—I looked over my shoulder at the staring faces of the others— "fare," I ended, copying his words.

"There are a number of secrets within this wood. I believe two areas are of particular interest."

I glanced at Mazrith. "Are you able to moor the boat?"

His expression tightened, possibly with hope. "There are no shores here. Frima, Svangrior, there is a slim chance we will need to linger inside the tree."

Both fae groaned. "Why?"

"We need to look for something."

"Maz, you can't take anything from the sacred tree of life," Frima said, horror in her voice.

"You know I would not. Can you use your shadows to bind the ship to the statue of Thor?"

I looked around at the endlessly high wooden bark walls, nothing but the five Court gates set into them, and the ring of statues surrounding the central waterfall. In my vision, the staircase had been between two gates. Was there a hidden level further up that held the chest I'd seen?

"Maz, it doesn't feel right to touch the statues like that," Frima said. She was frowning, staring up at Thor uncomfortably.

I looked back to Voror. "Are there any shores here? Hidden? Or places we could moor the boat?"

The owl clicked his beak. "Yes. There are rings in the walls."

"Really? Mazrith, Voror says there are rings in the walls."

We all stared at the sheer bark on the outer wall, between the Ice Court gates and the Earth Court gates.

Voror fluffed his wings, sighed into my mind, and took off. "Human eyesight is poor, but the fae should be able to see them," he muttered. When he reached the wall, he moved to a few feet above the water and gripped something in his talons. From where I was standing it just looked like bark, and I gasped as a large wooden ring rose from the wall.

"It was camouflaged," muttered Mazrith.

He maneuvered the boat quickly, and Frima's shadows swirled from her staff and wrapped around the ring, which once flat against the wall became almost invisible again.

"Where to, Voror?"

"There are runes carved into the toe of the statue of Odin."

"What do they say?"

He blinked at me. "My skills are extensive and magnificent, but they do not extend to reading."

I gave him an apologetic smile. "Maz, we need to go to the Odin statue."

"Svangrior. The *karve*."

The warrior and the Prince moved to the trapdoor into the hull of the ship, and between them hauled out a small boat, barely big enough for the hulking Prince. He dropped it into the water, then before I could say a word, lifted me by the waist and then over the railings. The tiny boat wobbled as my feet hit the bottom, and I dropped quickly into a crouch to stabilize it. Mazrith's weight joined me, and then we were moving, toward the statues.

It was so quiet inside the tree that I daren't say anything to Mazrith that the others would hear. But surely he would have to give them some sort of explanation for all this?

Voror flew overhead and landed on the left foot of the Odin statue. Mazrith guided our little boat to him.

The inscription was barely bigger than my fingernail,

but it was in the ancient language. I could read none of it. "How did you find this?" I gaped at the bird. "It's tiny."

He ruffled his feathers smugly. "My excellent scouting skills."

"Of course."

"It is another riddle," whispered Mazrith.

I stifled a groan. "Does it spell anything?"

"No, it is simpler than the others. *I run forever, but do not move at all, I have no lungs or throat but a roaring call.*"

"An animal?"

"No, it can't be. Animals move and have lungs."

"*It is a waterfall.*" I looked at Voror, then repeated his very smug words to Mazrith.

Slowly, we both looked at the epic waterfall behind the statues.

Frima didn't even want to touch the statue with her shadows, and now we were clambering over it like it was some sort of child's adventure area. I wasn't as suspicious as most fae, but it still felt wrong.

The spray of the water was cool on my face as we reached the other side of the statue, a very narrow ledge creating a ring that joined the back of all the statues together, around the waterfall.

"Rings of statues were popular with the gods, I guess." The waterfall was magically quiet, but there was enough noise trickling from it that I thought our voices would be masked from the others.

The waterfall itself was circular, as though it were being poured over a tube at the very top. "How do we get through it? In the *karve*?"

Mazrith shook his head. "No, I think it would tip immediately." He looked at me. "We swim."

I stared at him in alarm. "I won't be able to touch the bottom here."

"I will not let you drown."

Mazrith wasted little time taking off his fur cloak and laying on the ledge, before easing into the water. "It is warm. Come."

I took off my own cloak, then less confidently slid into the water. I groped for him straight away, kicking at the water to try to keep myself upright.

He held out one arm as he floated easily, taking my weight. "Hold your breath when we go under the fall."

"Okay," I panted, already getting tired.

He began to swim and I kicked my legs as I clung on. As we neared the gushing water, I realized that its volume was deceptive. The power behind the rushing water was plentiful, waves rolling against us as we got close.

"Will it force us under?" I gasped.

"Perhaps. Do not let go of me, whatever happens."

32

REYNA

Before I could stall or object, he kicked his legs hard and took us through.

The weight of the waterfall was massive. I was able to get one big breath before we were shooting down, forced by the impossible strength of the water. I squeezed my hand around Mazrith's arm as we tumbled and turned, trying desperately to catch him with my other. My fingers started to loosen as we turned, then I felt a strong hand grab my shoulder. With a jerk, we were pulled free of the downward current. Every instinct in me wanted to gasp for breath. I didn't know which was up or down, but then we were moving again, fast. Mazrith was kicking us to the surface.

I kicked with him, though I didn't think I was adding much, and mercifully we burst through the surface just seconds later. I chugged down air as I clung to Maz, blinking around, praying we had at least made it out on the other side of the waterfall.

We had. A disc stood in the center of the space inside the waterfall, with a pedestal on it. From our low view in the water, I couldn't see what was on it. Mazrith swam toward the disc, moving me to the side and then pushing my backside to help me clamber up and out of the water.

I was too shaken from the swim to appreciate his touch as anything more than lifesaving.

"Thank Freya you can swim so well," I breathed hard.

He made short work of using his strong arms to heave himself up and out gracefully, then pushed his hair out of his face as he stared up and around the space.

I looked up too. The ceiling was so high it was invisible. We must have been in the very center of the tree, the vein that ran directly through the middle of the colossal trunk. The soft light came from the sparkling water still cascading down all around us, except now I couldn't hear it at all, not even the soft trickling from before.

I looked at the pedestal, and my breathing stilled.

There was golden tree, a foot tall and made in the image of the tree of *Yggdrasil*. A giant snake wrapped around its trunk, and instead of five gates around the base, there were eight. Inscriptions in ancient runes ran out like roots from its base.

"What do they say?"

"There is one for each Court," Mazrith murmured as he moved around the pedestal to read them all.

"And the other three?"

"One for the dwarves... One for the Vanir... and one for the Fenrir."

"Fenrir? Aren't they wolves?" I remembered scary stories told between the children of the palace about the ancient wolf creatures, led by the fearsome Beowulf.

"Yes. They are as extinct as the dwarves and Vanir though."

"The three faceless statues in the shrine — do you think these are them?"

"Yes, probably."

I started to ask Voror and realized that there was no way he would have gotten through the waterfall. I hadn't heard him speak to me, either. Touching my headband, my stomach sank. His feather wasn't there. It must have been dislodged by the waterfall.

"There is one more inscription here." Mazrith pointed at runes that ran along the serpents back, tiny and intricately carved. He stared intently at it, then his eyes moved to mine. They were blazing with intensity. "This is it. Why you had to be a gold-giver," he whispered.

"What?"

"It says, 'send the serpent home'."

I blinked at him, then the golden tree. "What?"

"I think you need to change it. So that the serpent is moving toward the Shadow Court gate."

"Are you sure that is its home?"

He gave me a long look.

"Okay. Yes. It probably is." I took a deep breath. I wasn't in the best shape for working with gold, but I couldn't deny that it looked like that was what we were supposed to do.

"I don't have any tools," I said, crouching to look at the rest of the pedestal, in case there was anything there that I could use.

"What do you need?"

"My whole kit, ideally, but at the least something sharp, and something smooth, and something heavy."

"Do you have your finger talons?"

I pushed my hand into the pocket of my wet trousers and pulled out two. "Yes. That's something sharp."

He moved his hand to his hair, then pulled a large bead from one of his braids. It was silver, and when I took it from him I felt how perfectly smooth and round the surface was.

"That will work. Now something to bash the gold, to reshape it," I murmured.

This time his hand went to his neck. Shifting through four or five leather thongs, he selected one and pulled it over his head. A heavy amulet, in the shape of an hourglass, intricate snakes looping around each other carved into it. "Will that do for your needs?"

It had angles on each corner, and enough weight. "Yes, I think so. I don't know how long this will take," I told him. "Will Frima and Svangrior be alright for longer inside the tree? Will you?"

His eyes narrowed. "Yes. We do not become ill, or anything like that. We become..." He cast around for the right word. "Wild."

"Wild?"

"Instincts take over. Self-control is harder to exert. The magic of this place is intoxicating for fae."

"Oh. I see." That must have been why the king brought Tait here, I thought. "I'll get started then."

After so long without working with gold, I felt a gut-deep sense of rightness when the yellow-tinted vision dropped over my own. Runes floated from the metal, and I fell into them, letting them guide me. First, I carefully loosened the snake from his current position, letting the instructions come to me as I needed them. I tilted him, changing his angle, placing his fragile head at the gates to the Shadow Court. My makeshift tools weren't ideal, but wearing the sharp talons on my fingers actually sped up the work where I would usually have used a scalpel.

I had no idea how long I worked, but when the gold vision lifted, the snake had been reformed, hopefully heading for home.

Weariness washed through me, followed by stomach-tightening dread. The visions would come now. But I felt ready for them. I had no desire at all to see the Elder again, but last time I was sure she had tried to speak to me.

Perhaps I could be brave enough to try to learn something from her.

I sat cross-legged on the disc, Mazrith watching me cautiously. "What would you like me to do?"

"Nothing. It'll be over quickly."

There was a sudden grating sound, followed by whooshing and the sound of bark and twigs breaking.

Mazrith looked up, alarmed, but the ring of falling water

around us hadn't changed. I started to speak, but darkness dropped over my eyes.

I waited for the shadows, the dankness, the sense of something wrong. The scent of lilies washed over me, and a pair of gold eyes flashed in the gloom.

My breath hitched as the vision lifted, but I kept my eyes closed. I already knew I wouldn't see a Starved One next.

The second wave came, a roar of anger filling my ears. Mazrith and his mother were the only things visible in the darkness, the metallic tang of blood in the air. The vision lifted, and I ground my sweaty palms together.

I had no right to see this. This was his past, not mine.

The third wave came, and I was closer to them both. Now I could see the dagger in the woman's chest, plunged in her heart.

And Mazrith's fingers wrapped tight around it as he bellowed with rage.

My hands shook as the vision lifted.

No fourth, no fourth, no fourth. I had already seen more than I wanted to.

But darkness descended once more. And this time, Mazrith looked at me. Whether it was in the vision, or real life, my heart stopped beating.

He wasn't the Mazrith I knew.

He wasn't even the scarred Mazrith I had seen in the cave when he'd been injured.

Scarred didn't come close. As before, they covered every inch of his skin, but they were deep and raw, blackened on the edges. The skin beneath the scars was mottled and twisted, patches of swirling inky black bleeding across puckered flesh so white it could have been chalk. His face was feral, his eyes switching between gleaming gold and as black and soulless as the Starved Ones.

The vision lifted and I gasped for breath. I scrambled to my feet, my heart beating too fast.

I blinked at Mazrith in a daze.

"You killed your mother."

His concerned expression hardened like stone.

"And... I saw you," I mumbled thickly. "The real you."

The color drained from his face.

"You're not a shadow-fae." I knew it as surely as I knew I was rune-marked. "You're a gold-fae."

RAIDHO
JOURNEY
PROGRESS · GROWTH · THE PATH

THANKS FOR READING!

Thank you so much for reading Court of Monsters and Malice, I hope you enjoyed it! The cliffs are getting steeper, I know. And I'm only a little bit sorry. It'll be worth it, I swear.

The story continues in the next book, Court of Serpents and Secrets.

If you want to see some exclusive artwork of Maz and Reyna's dream, you can sign up to my newsletter at elizaraine.com. And maybe don't open it in company!